I0594496

SHIMMER

SUMMER'S HAREM BOOK 1

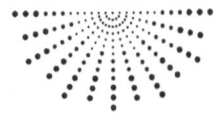

MAGGIE ALABASTER

CHAPTER ONE

"*F*or the millionth fucking time, don't call me Gardenia." What did I want to do more right now, slap him or screw him silly?

"It's your name, isn't it?" Huon smirked like the smug prick he was.

"Not for the last hundred years." I crossed my arms over my chest to keep myself from trying to wipe the expression off his face.

The door opened beside us and Sorrel peered out. "Keep it down." She glared at us both, then sighed deeply. "It won't be long now."

I dropped my hands to my sides. "Sorry." I glanced at Huon, but he was looking toward his feet.

He was a pain in my ass, but I understood his

reluctance to face the situation. Sooner or later, he'd have to.

"Summer, the king wants to see you." At least Sorrel used the name I chose for myself. She shot Huon an apologetic glance and waved me inside.

King Birch was an uncle to me in every way but by blood. Huon, his oldest son, would be king after him, but Birch always had a soft spot for me.

"Hey," I said softly.

The room was dark. Only a sliver of late afternoon sun dared to slip between the curtains and slant across the bed. The faint light was barely enough to illuminate the shell of the Fae who led us for the last two hundred years.

He smiled at me. In spite of the sickness, his expression was warm.

"Has Huon been calling you Gardenia again?" Of course he would think of anyone but himself in his final hours. That was just like him.

I flushed, embarrassed. "You heard?" He didn't need our childish arguments now. Okay, ever, but especially now.

"Yes." His voice was soft, laboured, but clear. Anyone else would have succumbed by now, let the sickness take them. Not Birch. He would fight until the last. "But I could tell by the look on your face." His eyes smiled as they did whenever he teased me.

I lightly touched my heated cheek. "He knows I hate it."

Birch chuckled, but it turned into a wheeze. He was too proud for me to fuss, so I stayed near the door.

"Huon can be a handful," he said finally. "As can you." His white teeth flashed.

"No Fae is perfect," I replied tartly. That was followed by a grimace. "Except Zinnia." My eldest sister was the epitome of grace and elegance, all the things I didn't give a shit about.

"It's you I've asked for, not her," Birch replied.

I knew that tone. It put me immediately on my guard. "What?"

"I want to ask one last thing," he said, totally guileless as always.

I resisted the urge to fly the hell out the window. For the second time in a handful of minutes, I crossed my arms over my chest.

"I'm not marrying Huon—"

"While I would like it if you did, it's not that." Birch paused. "I have another task for you. I want you to restore lesser magic to the Fae realm."

Yep, I should have left when I got the chance.

"Are you . . . Out. Of. Your. Fucking. Mind?" I asked.

He smiled again, tired, but full of charm. "I've never been more in my right mind."

"That's debatable." I moved over to perch on the side of his bed. The breeze from the open window caressed my wings. It tickled. I shifted position, turned my back away from the draught.

"All right, assuming I plan to buy into this crazy plan, where would I even start.?"

"Summer, Summer, Summer," he said slowly, "if anyone would know such a thing, it would be you."

"And yet," I said, "here I sit, lacking a clue. No one knows why lesser magic failed in the first place." I narrowed my eyes at him. "Right?"

When he didn't respond, I sighed. "I know you like puzzles, but if you know something, now is the time to say so." Or he could be infuriating, die and leave me with no answers and an impossible task. Fae aren't immortal, but we're stubborn and we live long enough to spend a few decades on a problem and get nowhere.

"Better yet, give this task to Huon. He could use something to pass the time for a century or so."

"His isn't the right magic for this, but combined—"

What?

"What?" I stared at him. "Combined how?"

"I'm not certain," he admitted. "I know there's an answer to this. Somehow. If you don't find it, Fae kind will die out."

There it was, he dumped the whole thing—guilt trip and all—on me.

"There might be no way to fix it. If higher magic can't do it, maybe nothing can," I pointed out.

"I'm certain there's a way. Higher and lesser magic aren't that different."

Truthfully, calling them that is a misnomer. What we call higher magic comes from us Fae. Lesser magic comes from the Earth itself. Whoever coined the terms was arrogant to decide our magic was more than that of the whole fucking planet, but it caught on. The distinction isn't relevant, as much as the fact there is one. The failure of natural magic was always going to be a disaster.

The problem was, in spite of what he said, I had no idea how to fix it.

"I need you to work with Huon." His voice was weaker now.

"Is the pain that bad?" I asked gently.

"Because it's making me delusional?" He gave me a faint smile.

"I don't want to be horrible, but I'm not ruling it out." The smile I gave back was watery. "Huon has never taken anything seriously in his life." I regarded Birch for a while. "That's the point, isn't it? You think whatever this task involves, it might make him grow up. Do you really think we have a chance?"

I might be difficult in many ways myself, but I was not a rehabilitation centre for wayward Fae. If that was what Birch was after, I was out.

"I know you can do this," he replied. "It's too late for me, but the rest of the Fae need you to do this, before it's too late for them."

"No pressure." I sighed. I wished he hadn't fallen sick with the wasting disease not even high magic could remedy. Birch could have gone on being king. Huon could take another few hundred years to mature.

It's true what they say, sometimes life makes you grow up too fast.

"I wish I didn't have to pressure you," Birch replied. "Give Huon a chance." He glanced toward the door. "I know he's been difficult—"

I snorted but didn't bother to disagree.

"He's also trying to find his place in the worlds," Birch finished.

I frowned. "He's a prince. The heir." I didn't add

that he would be king soon, the words hung in the air.

"That's a role," Birch said patiently, "it doesn't define him. What kind of king will he be? How will he rule? Those are things he has yet to work out."

"He needs more time," I whispered. A tear trickled down my cheek.

"There is no more time," Birch replied. "Like it or not, he will need your help. I wish..."

"Don't say it," I urged. "I wouldn't have wanted to be queen, even if I was related to you by blood."

He smiled wanly. "Of course not. The best monarchs are ones who didn't want the job."

"In that case, Huon will exceed all expectations," I said dryly.

"Perhaps, but I still need you to do this task for me. For Huon, for all the Fae."

I sighed again. "You know I will, even if it's against my better judgement to keep trying."

He reached for my hand and squeezed it. "I knew you would. You might not think you can do this, but you can. You won't be alone. There are others who will help you."

He exhaled and his hand relaxed. For a moment I thought he'd gone, but then he asked, "Can you tell

Huon to come in now? It's time to say goodbye to him."

"Of course." I leaned over to kiss his cheek. His skin was cool. Not quite icy, but not the warmth I was used to from him. "Safe travels through the seven hells." I didn't know whether or not there was such a thing, but I would have preferred him to stay in *this* life.

Birch nodded. "I'll see you again some day, if the gods allow."

I sniffed and hurried out the door. I only glanced back once, but it was through a sheen of tears.

"He wants to see you."

Huon nodded. His face was wet too, but he turned away as I appeared in the doorway. Any other time, I would have called him out on his pride. Today, I put a hand on his arm, patted it with my fingertips and moved away.

I had no more words to say, not yet.

CHAPTER TWO

"You think he was crazy, don't you?" Huon asked.

I reclined on an oversized leaf. My glistening wings stretched out under me to catch the rays of sun which peeked through the canopy of fragrant flowers over my head.

Huon flopped down beside me and made the leaf rock.

I put out a hand to steady myself. His use of 'was' left me breathless for a moment. Birch died peacefully four days ago, but it still hurt like a punch to my heart.

"No," I replied finally. "I think he was hopeful, optimistic and wanted the best for us all." Crazy? Maybe a little bit, but that was beside the point now.

"You know what he wanted for us," Huon said softly. "Apart from looking for lesser magic."

I looked into his eyes of brilliant blue. He had long lashes, even for a Fae, a broad mouth and strong chin. Most of that was from his mother. His nose was definitely from Birch.

"We fight like siblings," I pointed out.

"When we don't fuck like trolls," he added. Given the rate trolls bred, it was fortunate they only lived for a handful of years—just seventy or eighty or so.

He ran the tip of his finger down the side of my wing. One of the most sensitive places, as he well knew.

I shivered.

"Fucking doesn't make us suitable spouses." My mouth went dry.

"Why not?" He stroked his finger back up my wing.

"I can think of a dozen reasons." I should probably push him away, but I didn't want to. "What do you think of trying to get lesser magic back? Seriously."

He paused mid-stroke and looked me in the eyes. "If he thought it was possible, then I guess it is. It's worth a try anyway, right?"

I narrowed my eyes at him. "How many lovers

did you have in the human realm?"

He laughed softly. "Probably as many as you. Why? Are you jealous?"

I snorted. "Hardly." Fae weren't given to jealousy when it came to our mates. Huon's mother, Aster, had three husbands and I never saw Birch bothered by it for a moment.

"Good. Father seemed to think you're the key to bringing back lesser magic."

I nodded. "Something about combining magic. We never figured out what caused it to fail in the first place, so I have no idea what we'd try, combined or not."

"If you did know, would you do it?" he asked. "No matter what it was?"

I ran a hand over my hair and tugged lightly at the ends. That seemed like a simple question, but the gods only knew what sacrifice we might have to make.

"Yes, I would," I said finally. "We've both seen what's happening in the Fae realm. The plants are starting to die, the weather is different." At first the change was slow, barely noticeable, but now— I saw it more and more. Never without a shiver of fear.

Huon nodded. "We need to find the source of the problem first. At my father's suggestion, I asked a couple of my friends to help." He looked as though he had more to say, but didn't.

"You have friends who have time to do more than laze about drinking elderberry wine?" I teased.

He laughed softly. "The lifestyles of the bored and idle Fae. I certainly need to find more things for us to do." He cocked his head at me. "For example, what are you doing right now?"

I smiled. "Taking a break from picking berries." I showed him my hands, stained with juice.

His eyes on mine, he leaned to run his tongue up between two fingers before he took one between his lips and sucked gently. "Delicious. Just like the rest of you."

I looked at him through my lashes. "We really should be trying to find a solution to the problem of how to bring back lesser magic."

He smiled at me. "Afterward." He let go of my finger and leaned further over to tickle my neck with the tip of his tongue. His touch was barely more than a brush of a dragonfly wing, but it sent heat right to my core.

I swallowed, breathless already. "I guess it's waited for this long, it can wait a little while longer."

"Mmmhmm," he murmured. His breath brushed my neck. He slipped a hand down my leg and under my skirt, then back up my thigh. A light brush back and forth, he ghosted his fingers over the front of my panties, teasing my already aching pussy.

A huffed out a breath of need and felt him smile against my neck. He might be a prick, but he knew how to get me going.

"So hot for me already," he whispered.

Asshole.

He tugged my panties aside and slid a finger across my pussy. Then two, sliding over my already damp folds and around my needy clit. He teased like that for a while, his hard cock pressed against the side of my leg.

"Tell me you want me," he whispered insistently.

I wanted to tell him to fuck off, that I wouldn't beg. My pussy had other ideas. She wanted him right fucking now.

"I want you." I closed my eyes. "Please."

"Good girl," he soothed.

Gods, I should have hated that, but I didn't. Those words from between his lips were like a burst of fire right through me. The prick knew it too.

He found my clit and started to rub softly, gently. His skin barely touched mine, but it was enough to make me drenched and panting.

I hadn't even started to move against him when

he withdrew his hand.

"Take your panties off. They're in the way."

I glanced at him, frowning lightly, but raised my hips, pulled off my panties and tossed them aside.

"Skirt too," he added. "Off."

I undid my skirt and threw it in roughly the same direction as my panties.

"Now your top." He watched me through half-lidded eyes. "Now."

I drew my top over my head, careful not to pull my wings up with it. and it joined the small pile.

He smiled and sat back to admire my bared breasts. "I always forget how lovely you are," he said, his voice low and husky. "I could gobble you up." Instead, he lowered his mouth to one of my pert nipples. He traced circles around it with his tongue, then drew it between his lips and started to suckle, just hard enough to hurt. His teeth grazed my sensitive flesh, leaving red marks behind.

He cupped my ass and pulled me closer to him, before pressing his other hand back between my legs. He pushed my thighs apart and slid a finger inside me, then two. He stroked me from the inside, while the heel of his hand rubbed my clit.

"Free my cock," he said softly. "I want to feel your hand on me."

I only hesitated for a moment before I let my hand wander down to the hard bulge in his pants. I rubbed my palms across it once, twice, until he grunted.

"My cock in your hand, now."

Rough, like his tone, I tugged the laces of his pants undone and pulled them down to free his thick erection.

I wrapped my fingers around his length and slid them up and down in rhythm with my rocking against his hand.

"Fucking gods, Sum," he breathed.

"Now you remember to call me that," I teased.

He chuckled. The sound and his touch drove me closer to the edge. I bucked harder, needing release.

"That feels so good."

Underneath us, the leaf rocked with our movement, threatening to toss us off.

"Of course it does," he said, expertly working my g-spot and clit, while his hips thrust him harder into my hand. "Do you want to come?"

I could barely do words right now, so I murmured my agreement.

His hand stilled. "You know what I need to hear."

I growled softly in frustration, but all he did was laugh.

"Not until you ask."

I gritted my teeth and said nothing until he started to pull his hand away.

"Please," I said quickly. "I want to come." Asshole loved it when I begged. Secretly, so did I. This thing between us, this game, it made us both hot.

"Good girl," he said approvingly. He went back to working me, harder than before. Hard enough to blur the line between pleasure and pain. Maybe they were the same thing.

"Prick," I said in response, but I rode his hand for all I was worth, letting him bring me to edge and over, release flooding through me and out, coating his hand.

I screamed with sheer pleasure. My hand tightened around his cock.

He bucked, pounding in and out of my curled fingers.

"Fuck." His voice was ragged. "I'm going to cream your wing."

He turned at an angle, taking my hand with him.

He drove himself harder and harder. His wet tip made my hand slick, but I kept my grip. I watched his face through half-lidded eyes. His were open, brow creased in concentration.

After a minute, two minutes, he gave a grunt,

then a groan. He bucked hard against my hand before squirting his cum all over my extended wing.

The burst of hot, wet, cream on such a sensitive place nearly made me come again.

"Not without asking," he said before I could. "Don't you dare."

He flopped and gasped a few breaths before he pressed his hand deeper into me. Each stroke drove me higher and higher.

"Please," I begged, "I need to come. Please." I didn't even bother to argue with him this time. If I didn't come, I might have ignited.

When the second orgasm flooded over me, I threw my head back and screamed out, "Huon! Oh, the gods..."

The ecstasy washed me away for a minute, two minutes, lost in a world of pure pleasure. I could have stayed locked there forever.

Eventually, the sensation faded, leaving behind a feeling of languid satisfaction.

I flopped back onto the leaf and let my breath return in its own good time.

"You see why we're such a good team?" Huon asked softly.

I opened my eyes a crack and exhaled. "Sex and love aren't the same thing." We'd had that conversation at least as many times as I told him not to call me Gardenia.

This time, he actually looked hurt. He turned his face away while he pulled up his pants.

Was it even possible he felt *that* way about me? I had no idea. He never took anything seriously long enough for me to see what he was really thinking.

I sat up and put a hand on his arm. Underneath his clothes, he was firm and muscular. His wings jutted out of openings in the back of his tunic and lay across the cotton fabric. They were much like mine, but darker, shot through with blues and purples.

"Was it something I said?" I kept my voice light. Had I missed subtle signals somewhere along the line? If that was the case, he was far too subtle for me. The fact I was using Huon and subtle in the same thought would have made me laugh under other circumstances.

He shrugged. "I guess not," he replied. "I mean, you're right. Sex is just sex. Just a bit of fun, right?"

"Yes," I agreed tentatively. "It usually is." I'd been in love once or twice. Intimacy meant more then, when strong emotions were tangled with lust. At least, for me it had, but those brief relationships ended a long time ago.

I opened my mouth to say something, but no more words came. I lowered my hand and moved away to dress.

"At least the leaf didn't give out this time," he said.

I looked up to see him smile at me, back to his usual self.

"Yes, thank the gods. Although last time was kinda fun." I pulled on my panties and skirt before I picked up my top and let it dangle from my fingers.

Hand on my hip, I asked, "Did you ever find your other boot?"

He chuckled. "No. Did you find your top?"

I grinned. "Luckily I did, but I'm kinda glad I don't have to go looking this time."

"Oh, I don't know. It might have been fun to search for it again." He wiggled his brows.

I looked down and shrugged. "It might cause a scandal if I walked around topless." He had, of course, given me his tunic that time. Silly how it was all right for men to wear no shirt, but not women.

"Probably." He wrinkled his nose. "Some Fae are such prudes."

Maybe I imagined his hurt a few moments ago. He seemed fine now, as far as I could tell. Men were confusing, even Fae ones. Particularly Fae ones.

"Especially my sisters." I tugged my top on and shook out my wings.

He grimaced. "There goes the mood." Laughter danced in his eyes.

I grinned. "Yes, but we really need to focus on magic and other things. You do have a realm to rule, after all."

The humour fled his face.

"You can't abdicate, if that's what you're thinking," I said quickly.

"I know," he sighed. "I just feel like I'm too young for this responsibility. I'm barely over a hundred years old."

"Poor baby," I teased. "So young, yet we still have to solve this problem."

He scratched his head. "I know someone I can ask to help us. Other than my frivolous friends."

"*Please* don't suggest my sisters." I made a face.

"I know better than to do that." He tied his pants and straightened the hem of his tunic. "Do you want to come for a swim in the river? I'll introduce you afterward."

When I started to remind him of our task, he added, "I know what we need to do, but it's waited this long. It can wait another hour."

CHAPTER THREE

*T*he 'river,' was a slow moving creek, but at our size, it was wide and deep.

My favourite place to swim was under a bower of roses. When they were in full bloom, they dappled the sunlight and made the place both private and fragrant.

Right then though, they were coming to the end of their season. Patches of brown dotted here and there.

"Before lesser magic failed, they never stopped blooming." I stepped out of my clothes and into the water.

"I remember." Huon looked somber as he too tossed his clothes aside.

I admired the corded muscles in his arms, his

narrow waist leading down to that delicious V, his defined stomach and chest. He shook out his wings and waded in behind me.

He must have noticed me looking, because he grinned.

Prick.

I shook my head at him and dove in deeper. The water was cold, but clean and clear. Where the light penetrated, the bottom of the river was visible; a mixture of sand and brightly coloured pebbles. Blues and greens and yellows.

I popped out into the air and let the water pour off my face and hair.

"Watch out!" Huon's warning shout made me turn.

Shit.

A large, white rose petal floated directly toward me. Even at half the size of the leaf we'd lain on, it was huge to a tiny Fae, big enough to knock me aside. Trust me, these things are deceptively soft. When you're this small, they suck, big time.

I glanced up quickly. If I made myself human-sized, I would break through the bower and destroy several Fae's hard work. My wings were too wet to fly me out of the way.

Okay, time for the big guns, so to speak.

I curled my hands into fists, my nails pressing into my palms, and summoned magic from deep inside me.

At first, I didn't think it was going to respond in time. A spike of panic rose, but I shoved it aside. I had no time for that. Not now. I could freak out later.

Finally, up it surged. The pure, sweet pulse of power singing through my blood.

I opened my hands and threw a shimmering blast of golden magic at the petal.

It struck the edge and glowed for a heartbeat, two heartbeats.

Then it exploded.

Tiny, soggy pieces of petal flew in every direction. The water erupted. The force sent a wave across the surface of the river.

It washed over me and knocked me off my feet. Arms, legs and wings flailing, I was tossed ass over head until I wasn't sure which way was up.

Frantic, I held my breath until something gripped my arm and pulled me to the surface. I gasped for air.

Vaguely aware of dark wings, I let myself be pulled to the riverbank and deposited there on the sand. I coughed up a mouthful of water. Then another.

Fucking petal.

I started on my third as Huon was dumped down beside me.

He coughed too, but didn't look any worse for wear.

"Maybe less magic next time," a new voice remarked.

I looked up. Dark wings, dark eyes, dark skin. After a hundred years, I had met most Fae, although some kept to themselves in other parts of the Fae realm. This was a face I hadn't seen in dozens of years.

"Or duck *under* the petal," Huon said helpfully.

I ignored him and cleared my throat. "Thank you —" I tilted my head and waited for him to give his name.

"Kale," he supplied, his voice a deep rumble that went straight to my pussy. "I was sent from my village to find the king." His gaze swept over my body before moving to Huon.

"You found him," Huon said. "Just in time too." He rose and offered Kale his hand as though he wasn't naked and looking like a drowned troll.

I used my magic, more carefully this time, to

bring my clothes over to me. A little finger-full was all I needed to float them above the sand to my outstretched hand.

"What brings you here?" Huon asked pleasantly.

While they talked, I dried my skin and dressed, then wrung out my hair.

"You're trying to restore lesser magic," Kale said simply, not wasting a word.

"You've come to help?" Huon sounded surprised. His eyes flicked to me and widened as though he wondered when I'd dressed.

"We could use it." I walked over to pick up his pants and toss them to him.

He nodded his thanks and pulled them on. "Summer is right, we could use all the help we can get."

Kale gave me a nod. His eyes seemed to drink in the sight of me.

The feeling was mutual. Muscles bulged from his sleeveless tunic. Unlaced part way down his chest, it revealed firm skin with a smattering of hair. His pants clung to his thighs, defining yet more muscle there. And his wings... They made my breath catch in my throat.

"Then I'm at your disposal." His faint smile was

for me alone, until it faded and he turned back to Huon.

"Excellent." Huon seemed oblivious to the looks that passed between Kale and I. "We were just about to meet with a friend of mine to discuss it. You're welcome to join us."

Kale nodded. "Very well."

Huon picked up his own tunic, shook sand from it and pulled it over his head. "So, which village are you from?" he asked, his voice muffled by fabric.

"Springblade."

When he didn't elaborate, Huon nodded and tugged his hem down. "That's in the east, isn't it?"

"East south-east," Kale replied simply.

"On the coast?" I'd studied the maps. I had a fair idea of where most places in the realm were. The inhabited places anyway. And I wanted to hear Kale talk more.

"Yes."

Maybe I was hoping for too much. I exchanged glances with Huon. He shrugged. Not everyone was as talkative as him.

"So, who is this friend we're meeting up with?" I asked.

He tilted his head. "Wait and see," he teased.

I rolled my eyes and said to Kale, "He's always like this. It's a wonder anything ever gets done."

He gave me another faint smile, which made my heart skip. If he was going for mysterious, he was succeeding.

"I have that same wonder," Huon said lightly, and grinned. "But here we are."

"Doomed?" I joked.

"Hey, who almost blew up the river and drowned us both?"

I had the grace to flush. "I haven't had to do that before."

"The Fae aren't trained in magic here in the capital?" Kale asked.

"Of course," I replied, "just not in blowing up rose petals on water. Who would have anticipated that being a problem?"

Kale glanced up at the bower. He said nothing, but I saw what he was thinking. Anyone who swam under roses should be prepared for them to drop parts of themselves into the river. Lucky it wasn't a thorn.

"The loss of lesser magic is making them deteriorate," I said softly. "It wasn't a problem before. But now—"

"Now it almost got us killed," Huon finished.

"Who knows what other hazards we might have to deal with until we get it fixed?"

"We need to be more vigilant," I agreed.

"And work swiftly," Kale said.

"Saff might have some answers." Huon spread his wings. They caught the sun and shimmered like brightly coloured cellophane.

"Ah-ha, that's who we're meeting." I followed his example and gave mine a shake to be sure they were dry. Damp wings would drag me down.

Kale cocked his head at Huon. "Saff?

"Saffron," Huon replied. Now he was the one being cagey. "He's been... traveling."

I waited for him to say more, but instead, he leapt into the sky and headed toward the castle, leaving us to hurry after him.

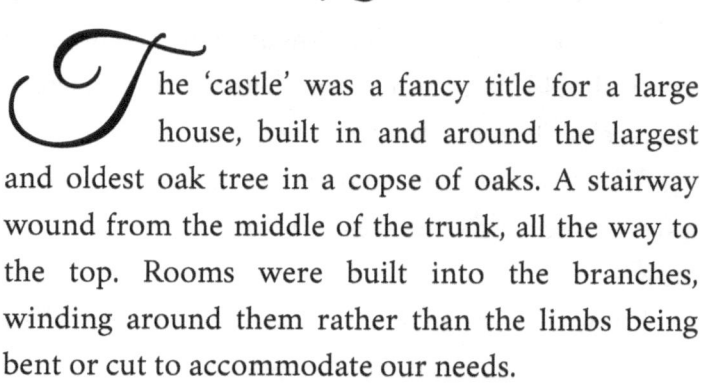

The 'castle' was a fancy title for a large house, built in and around the largest and oldest oak tree in a copse of oaks. A stairway wound from the middle of the trunk, all the way to the top. Rooms were built into the branches, winding around them rather than the limbs being bent or cut to accommodate our needs.

It was high enough to keep trolls out, and big enough to comfortably house a few hundred Fae.

A few thousand Fae occupied other oaks, while still others were scattered all across the realm.

The highest point of the castle served as a landing area, although a dozen balconies had enough room for a handful of us at once. While the regular residents—myself included—used the balconies closest to our rooms, it was considered rude for newcomers to land anywhere but the crown of the tree. Not even the king would break this tradition.

That didn't stop Huon from heading toward the stairs the moment he landed, forcing me to trot along behind him to catch up.

Asshole.

I glanced at Kale, but he didn't look bothered. His long legs ate up the distance, but he kept pace with me. If he thought Huon was rude, he showed no sign. In fact, his expression gave away nothing but a mild interest in his surroundings.

He must have noticed me looking, because he gave me a nod and gestured for me to walk down the stairs first.

"Are you worried I'll trip and fall on you?" I asked teasingly. After the incident at the river, he might have thought I was accident prone or dangerous.

"If you trip, I will be there to catch you," he said solemnly.

"Me too," Huon said from a few steps down.

"I'll be sure not to trip then." I lifted my chin and started down. I had *some* pride.

Having to be rescued once today was bad enough. Twice would be mortifying.

"I will too," Kale said.

I glanced back over my shoulder. His expression was deadpan; no hint of humour, although I was pretty sure he was joking.

"Good," Huon told him. "I'm not sure she could catch you unless she uses her magic, and you saw what that can do."

I grimaced to myself. I blow something up a grand total of once, and I'd hear about it for the next decade.

"I can use it on you, if you like," I said darkly.

He raised his hands in surrender. "Please don't."

"Fine, I won't," I said, "at least until after we get lesser magic back."

"I'm not sure that's the best incentive." He looked as though he'd say more, but we'd reached the upper hall, where kings and queens met their guests upon their arrival.

There, apparently waiting for us, was a Fae with

bright red hair. Unlike Huon and Kale, he wasn't muscular. Rather, he was tall and slender, as though he ran everywhere instead of flying. His eyes were golden brown and looked as full of humour as his wide mouth.

"Saff!" Huon hurried forward and offered his hand to the newcomer.

"Your highness." Saff shook his hand, then tugged him in for a hug, evidently not intimidated by Huon's new position. "I'm sorry for your loss."

Huon sighed as the joy faded from his face. "Thank you. We all miss my father's wisdom."

Saff nodded solemnly and said, "Yes, it's a shame he didn't pass it on."

After a beat or two, Huon laughed and punched him on the arm. "Let me introduce you to Summer and Kale."

Saff shook hands with Kale, but his eyes lingered on me. "I see why they call you Summer." He looked hungry, like a man who hadn't eaten in days. And I don't mean food. He wanted to taste me, all of me. The way his tongue swept over his lips made me wet.

"Because it's my name?" I suggested lightly. Yeah, I could tell where this was leading already and I was here for it.

"It's not *exactly* her name," Huon said. "She didn't like the one her parents gave her. So she changed it."

Saff's broad mouth broke into a warm smile. "Because she's hot? It suits her."

Yep, there it was. How many times today was I going to roll my eyes? I did it again now.

"Isn't she?" Huon said. His gaze raked me just as much as the rest of them, flicking to my wings and reminding me of the way his cum felt on my, warm and slippery.

I cleared my throat and crossed my arms over my chest. "Please don't talk about me like I'm not here. I changed it to Summer because it was my favourite season."

"Was?" Saff asked. The smile faded from his face, but his eyes stayed on me, along with his full attention.

I shrugged. "Since we lost lesser magic, it's been more humid. It's slowly killing the plants and flowers. How long will it be before they're all gone? If that happens, we will be next."

Saff nodded. "That's what I've seen all over the realm. Birch sent me to check along the northern expanses, to see if I could find a clue as to what's going on. I was hoping to be back before…" Was that a tear glistening on his lashes? He rubbed his face with one hand. When he lowered it, any hint of moisture was gone.

He shook his head and let his hand drop to his side with a light slap of skin on fabric. "If there was anything, I didn't find it."

"There's also no sign along the eastern coast," Kale said.

"That leaves the—" Huon stopped short and looked over my shoulder.

I grimaced.

"There you are, *Gardenia.*" Zinnia was immaculate in a long white dress with lace sleeves. Her delicate wings peered out the artfully tailored flaps at the back. She regarded me through long lashes, as though she smelled something disgusting. Even her hair was perfect, pinned in coils on her head.

I wanted to pull out all the pins, one by one, and mess up her hair, or maybe just tear it out. Just once, I'd like to see her put a stain of *something* on her perfect clothes. Preferably something dark, which didn't wash out.

Yeah, that sounds petty, but trust me, it's justified.

I pretended to inspect my fingernails. "A little busy here, Zinnie." She detested her childhood nickname as much as I hated mine. "Did you need something?"

She eyed the men around me. I could see her wondering why they were wasting their time. It was no secret she wanted to be queen some day. It was also no secret Huon couldn't stand her any more than I could.

Zinnia sniffed. "Mother wanted you to come home for dinner. She hasn't seen you in a while."

I immediately felt bad. She was right, I hadn't been to visit our parents in weeks. I had been busy, but I also didn't need them fussing over me. My sisters enjoyed the attention. Me—it just made me uncomfortable.

"Tell her I'll pop in tomorrow, if I have time."

Zinnia looked down her long nose at me. "Or you could tell her yourself."

I glanced over at Huon, sure he would be holding back a laugh. Instead, he looked annoyed.

"I need Summer here," he said in a clipped tone. "If your mother wishes, she can drop by, but not tonight. We have matters of importance to the realm to discuss."

"All the more reason she should get out of your hair." Zinnia's voice was sweeter than honeysuckle, but with an edge of venom. "You're far too busy to let Gardenia waste your time."

Huon's face turned pink, but it was me who spoke.

"That's up to the *king* to decide. Maybe you should mind your own business for once." Bitch.

She flinched, but then straightened up and rolled her eyes. Apparently it's a family trait, along with being stubborn and outspoken.

"I see. It wasn't enough to share the late king's bed. You need to wrangle your way into *this* king's bed as well."

The shocked silence which followed her words was broken by Huon's laugh.

"As if I need to be wrangled. I'm practically begging *her*." His eyes shone and he shook his head. "Look, I think you mean well—"

"Don't count on it," I said. "For the record, I never slept with Birch. He was like a father to me. A *second* father," I added quickly. My father was lovely but overrun by a wife and daughters who adored attention. I was the quiet one who was always self-sufficient and busy roaming about the Fae and human realm to satisfy my boundless curiosity.

When I wasn't doing that, I was reading. Birch had a much bigger library than the one at home.

Huon shrugged. "It wouldn't have been anyone's business if you had." He flashed an insincere smile at

Zinnia and took my arm. "It's time we ate and finished our conversation. We'll be sure to call on you if we need any help."

Zinnia opened her mouth, but for once nothing came out. She gave a curt nod, turned on her heel and stalked away.

CHAPTER FOUR

I groaned and patted my full belly. I'd eaten so much I might pop if I had another mouthful. The food here was always so good, especially when the palace had visitors and the cooks wanted to impress them.

Mushrooms cooked in garlic and wine and stuffed with rice and other vegetables were a particular favourite of mine. We'd also had roasted vegetables, and mashed ones, a soup made from sweet potatoes and a selection of cakes for dessert.

While Huon, Saff and I overindulged, the impressiveness of the spread seemed to be lost on Kale. He ate some bread and soup, but waved away everything else, even the wine.

Huon leaned over to refill my glass and sat back

to regard the three of us. "Now we're alone, we can get back to business."

I let the sweet wine sit on my tongue for a moment before I swallowed.

"Are you sure we shouldn't include everyone in this?" Saff asked. He managed to look serious for more than a minute or two. That was the perfect indication of how serious this was. I mean, we were potentially discussing the end of the world. If that wasn't a good time to be serious, when was?

Huon looked thoughtful, then shook his head. "We don't want to cause panic."

"Anyone with their eyes open will have noticed what's happening by now," Saff pointed out.

"Yes, but we can let them think we have this under control," Huon said with a firm nod that reminded me of his father.

My heart twinged with sadness. Birch should be here now, leading all of this, even if he also had no answers.

"We've faked it for this long," I said. "So what's next? The north and east don't seem to hold the key. Unless you've sent someone west, then I guess that's our next starting point?"

Huon nodded. "West is troll country; I was hoping to avoid going there."

"And south is the veil," Kale said.

"We've all been there," I said, "to try to get through or to help…"

Saff jerked. "Help what? Who?" He blinked furiously. "You're not saying—"

"Yes, I am," I replied reluctantly.

"How many?"

"Twenty or thirty, as far as anyone can tell."

Saff gaped. "Twenty or thirty Fae are stuck on the other side of the veil?"

"That or killed by trolls." I slowly turned my wineglass in my fingers. "At first we thought lesser magic would start working again and we could find out for sure."

"It's been *months*," Saff said breathlessly. He was clearly struggling to get his head around the idea of that many stuck, unable to get home. Honestly, I'd known for a while and still couldn't. All I could do was thank the gods it wasn't me, and try to find a way to get them back here. If there was a way. If not…

I couldn't meet his eyes. "I know. We *will* find a way to fix this and get them all home."

He nodded. "We have to. For all our sakes."

I reached over the table and patted his hand. My fingers lingered longer than might have been necessary, but touching him felt natural, like we'd done it a hundred times before.

He offered a smile in reply. I could tell he felt it too, it was written in his gaze, a combination of surprised and pleased.

Huon cleared his throat. "With that in mind, I'll be leaving my mother in my place."

I frowned at him. "Why?"

"Because we need to go west. I'm not sending people that way if I won't go myself."

"The Fae need our king—" I started.

"The Fae need strong leadership and the restoration of lesser magic," he said in a firmer tone than I'd ever heard him use. "This is the only way I can do both."

"This is how you might get killed," I said tersely.

"How can I get killed when I have you protect me?" he asked.

"Accidents happen," I muttered.

He laughed. "Besides, I also have these two fine Fae." He gestured toward Saff and Kale. His expression turned serious. "I've made up my mind. We leave tomorrow. Tonight you can take time to get to know each other better and then get some rest."

He raised his glass in a toast. "To us and our impending success."

Saff raised his glass, then Kale did the same a moment later. Reluctantly, I followed suit, then took a gulp.

Impending doom might be more accurate.

"Summer, gentlemen, I have to excuse myself. I need to speak with my mother." Huon put his glass aside and stood. "By all means, stay and keep drinking. I'll see you all on the crown in the morning." He gave us a bow and then left the room.

An awkward silence followed, then Kale also rose. "I have had a long journey. Goodnight." He nodded and headed out. My eyes followed him, brows knitted at his abrupt departure.

"That just leaves us then," Saff said.

I smiled. "About the Fae on the other side—"

"I know if there was anything which could have been done, it would have been by now," he said quickly. "We just have to keep trying to find a way."

"We will," I assured him. "We won't stop until we do."

He stared at me for a moment. "Do you want to get some air? It looks nice out on the balcony."

I hesitated before saying, "I could use some air." I preferred to be outside anyway, like most Fae, surrounded by nature. A part of it.

He offered me his hand and didn't let go when

we stepped through the doorway. It was dark outside, except for lights dotted in the rooms and houses around us. The night air was crisp and clear. A million stars dotted the sky, going on forever.

"Can I ask you something?"

"I suppose so," I replied warily. His hand felt nice in mine, warm and strong. I couldn't help imagining how they'd feel on my body. I knew he wanted to find out as much as I did.

"Do you believe in love at first sight?" he asked.

"I—I'm not sure. Why?"

"Well… I didn't used to," he said softly, "until I met you."

"I—"

He pressed a firm finger to my lips. "You don't have to say anything. I didn't mean to put you on the spot. Maybe it's the wine, but I wanted you to know how I feel." He paused and swallowed. "I'd like to kiss you. To taste you."

I took a shallow breath. "Why don't you?" I whispered.

He leaned in and pressed his lips to mine. His hand came up and tangled in my hair.

His mouth was warm and tasted of wine. I parted my lips and let his tongue sweep across my lips and slip into my mouth. I sucked the tip like it was his cock, drawing him in deeper until our teeth clashed.

He moaned. "I want you." He slipped his hands down my body, cupped my ass and pulled the length of my body to his.

His cock was hard through the thin layers of clothing between us. He pressed it against me, ground it, demanding more.

"I want you too," I said, his mouth muffling my words.

Without breaking the kiss, he manoeuvred us both until my back pressed against the wall. He slid his hands up under my top and over my belly. Gradually, he moved them up until his hand covered my breasts. His palms grazed my nipples, lightly at first, before he started to rub them firmer, making them pebble under his touch.

I moaned.

He gripped the hem of my top with one hand and tugged it upward. I helped him pull it over my head and toss it aside.

"Gods," he whispered, admiring my bare breasts in the starlight. "You're perfect."

He went back to work on my nipples, twisted and turned them gently with his fingertips, worshiping every millimetre of tender flesh.

I found the ties at the front of his trousers and worked them loose, my hands trembling with need. One push and they fell to his feet, freeing his cock whichwas bigger than I would have guessed, and curved slightly up toward my face.

He kicked his pants aside and pulled off my skirt and slid my panties down my legs. It was my turn to kick them aside before I helped him with his shirt.

I was right, he wasn't as buff as Huon and Kale, but he was still all chiselled muscle, rock hard, with curls of red hair around his cock.

He cupped my ass again, and picked me up. My back against the wall, his cock was pressed against my already drenched pussy.

With a grunt, and a single firm stroke, he slid his cock into my body. He stood still for a long moment, as though savouring the feel of me. Then he pulled out and slammed back into me. Over and over he pounded, relentless, needy. He held back nothing.

My breath was ragged. Every thrust drove me closer and closer to the edge.

"You feel so fucking good," he said into my ear.

"So do you." And he did. The way he filled me, it was like my body was made for him to fuck. And yet I wanted more.

Slowly, he drew out of me and carried me away

from the wall. He lay me down on the wooden slats that made up the balcony. He lay beside me and tickled my navel with his tongue.

I writhed and laughed softly. He looked up at me and smiled, white teeth flashing in the darkness.

He did it again, then started to slowly move up my body, kissing and licking as he went.

"You taste so good," he whispered.

"So I've been told," I replied lightly. Earlier that day too. Usually I wasn't quite so—loving, but I wasn't going to feel bad about it.

He wanted this, I wanted this, we weren't hurting anyone.

"Oh really?" he said teasingly. "I'll have to come up with some new lines then."

He reached my breasts and licked one nipple thoroughly before he gripped it lightly between his teeth. He watched me while he did it, to gauge my reaction.

I moaned.

He bit down a little harder, sending a zap of pleasure and pain all the way through me.

"Gods, yes." I writhed under his touch.

He moved over to bite down on my other nipple. If I wasn't dripping wet before that, I was now.

He grazed his teeth over my whole breast,

stopped here and there to kiss and lick and bite. I'd have marks from him after this. That thought was hot as hells. Like somehow he was making me his here and now.

His hand found my clit and he started rub roughly with two fingers while lavishing his attention on my breasts.

I arched my back and rode his hand hard, that spike of pleasure a heartbeat or two away.

"Come for me," he insisted. "I want to hear you."

Well, at least I didn't have to beg. I couldn't hold back either. I came so hard I screamed his name. Stars shattered in front of my eyes and were reborn. I might have shattered too. Before I fully came back together, he straddled me, nudged my legs apart with his knees and slammed his cock back into me.

Like before, he thrust hard and fast, putting everything into each stroke, every breath, every grunt, all the power in his hips.

"I'm going to come inside you," he said with ragged breath.

I reached around to cup his ass and lightly raked my nails over his skin. Then firmer.

"Ah yes, that will do it." He grunted and thrust faster and faster. A long, low moan escaped his lips and ended in a gasp, quickly followed by another. He stilled and poured his cum into me.

He collapsed, panting beside me.

"I have to say," he said once he was finally able to breathe again, "you're a nice surprise."

I lifted my head to look at him. "Now that's one I have never heard."

He sat up and rubbed his chin. "You should hear it often. I'll be sure you do."

"Charmer," I told him. I sat up beside him and leaned against his arm.

He laughed softly. "Now that's something *I've* never heard before."

"Oh, what do you usually hear?"

He breathed in and out through his nose. "Usually insults relating to the colour of my hair."

I touched his head lightly. "I like your hair."

"I like yours." He leaned over and kissed the top of my head. "I meant what I said."

"About what?" I let lethargy start to creep up on me and closed my eyes.

"What I said about love at first sight. Although," he added, "I think it happened before we met. After all the things Huon told me about you."

My eyes shot open. "He did what?" What the—

Saff chuckled. "He talks about you all the time. He's been head over heels for you for years."

I swallowed. "Is this going to be a problem between you two?" We had enough on our plate without this kind of drama. Maybe I should have thought twice before letting Saff fuck me.

"No, why should it? I care about you, he cares about you, neither of us mind. And if you feel the same way, then I don't mind sharing." He put an arm around me. "But that's up to you."

I frowned. "Wait a minute. How do you know he doesn't mind?"

"We talked about it. Why do you think he excused himself so early?"

What the hells?

"You two presumed a lot." I shifted away from him. A whole lot. Had Huon told Saff I'd be an easy fuck? If he did, I'd...

"Wait. No, it's not like that," he said quickly. "I only wanted time alone with you to talk."

"Was Kale in on this too?" I asked.

"No, him leaving then was just a bonus."

I wasn't sure I believed him. Right now I didn't care. I got up, hunted down my clothes and started to pull them on.

"Summer, please don't be angry. I had no idea it

would end like this, I swear. I wanted to get to know you, that was all. I mean, maybe the wine helped me to get a little carried away, but Huon and I didn't plan for you and I to make love."

"Love?" I spat. "You don't even *know* me. You might not even like me for all you know. Hells, I might not like you. It was just a meaningless fuck—"

"I'm sure if you gave it some time—"

I interrupted. "We'll have plenty of time when we travel to troll country." If I was speaking to him or Huon. Maybe Kale and I could be quiet together.

"I'm tired. I'm going to bed. Alone."

Before he could say anything else, I wrapped my arms around myself and stomped away.

He and Huon were both so infuriating I couldn't decide who I was angrier at. By the time I reached my room and slammed the door shut behind me, I'd decided to be mad at them both.

And myself for letting them play me like that.

Pricks.

CHAPTER FIVE

*W*hen we met on the crown in the morning, Huon didn't meet my eyes.

Asshole.

Saff tried, but I pointedly ignored him.

Kale gave me a nod and a faint smile, apparently oblivious to what happened the night before.

"You brought your pack, I see," Huon said.

I smirked at him as I slid it off my back and set it on the ground at my feet. "Your powers of observation are as good as ever."

"Summer—" He took a step toward me.

"Don't." I I held up my hands and moved away. "We should be worrying about the job we have to do. Nothing else matters right now."

"Your feelings matter," he said insistently. He put out a hand, but I ignored it.

"I'm a big girl, I'll deal with it." I didn't look at his face. I wanted to tell him to fuck the fucking fuck off, but the whole world was at stake, and that was more important than him setting me up, or me falling for it.

From the corner of my eye, I saw him drop his hand. Good. Maybe next time he'd think twice about talking about me behind my back. Or anyone else for that matter. Did we have time for me to give him a swift kick in the balls? That might have to wait until later.

I gave myself a mental shake and focused on the present, and what was important right now. That was definitely not his balls. Or his cock, which I didn't want to think about, even though it...

"We should go before we attract a crowd," I said. *And I get too distracted thinking about dick.*

"I still think we should take more Fae with us," Saff remarked. He gave Huon a meaningful look, as if they'd argued the point before I arrived.

"We need to be inconspicuous," Huon said. "Four is probably more than we should have."

He turned to me.

"You are *not* leaving me behind," I said before he could speak. "Birch wanted me to fix this."

"He wanted *us* to fix this." Huon shook his head. "Arguing will get us nowhere." He picked up his pack and swung it onto his back.

"At last, something we agree on." I picked up my own pack and tucked my wings in tight so I wouldn't put a strap over one. "Have you got a map?"

Huon smacked his forehead. "Now why didn't I think of that?" He grinned, pulled one out of his pocket and started to unfold it.

Smartass.

"Are the Fae here always like this?" Kale asked to no one in particular.

"What, lots of fun?" Saff asked.

Kale raised his eyebrows at him.

"I've only just met Saff, but *King* Huon has always been a featherbrain," I said sweetly.

Huon smiled at me. "It's just a part of my charm."

I snorted. "If you say so."

He gave an exaggerated sigh. "Some day she'll admit she loves me." Something flashed in his eyes but he turned and leapt off the crown before I could respond.

Saff shrugged and followed him.

"Maybe I should apologise in advance for both of

them," I said, "but they're old enough to take responsibility."

Kale chuckled. "In my village, very few Fae are
jokesters. It's... refreshing." He gave me a look which
made my heart flutter.

"I suppose it would be. It keeps life entertaining."
Even if Huon was an infuriating, arrogant pain in
my ass at the same time.

Kale nodded. "Shall we?" He offered me his hand.

Pulse thumping, I took it. His hand was large and
warm in mine, reassuring and somehow safe.

He nodded and we leapt, wings stretched to catch
the air before we soared after the other two.

~

We flew west for several hours before
Huon gestured for us to land.

He chose a copse in the middle of a stand of a
dozen kinds of trees. The moment his feet touched
the ground, he stopped and looked around, a
worried expression on his face.

It took me a few moments to realise what was
bothering him.

All around us, the trees bore brown. Not just the
natural brown of drying leaves I'd seen in the human

world. These trees looked as though they rotted where they stood.

And the smell.

I pinched my nose.

"I smelt rotten meat once." Huon's face was unusually serious. "That's what these smell like."

"Trees aren't made of meat," Saff pointed out. "Not usually anyway." He frowned at his own comment, as though trying to make sense of it. He quickly gave up.

I stepped carefully to the closest one, a beech, and lightly touched the leaves with my fingertips. They felt cold and moist. When I drew my hand back, chunks came away. Some of it coated my fingers. I rubbed my thumb against it.

My skin began to sting.

"Maybe don't touch them," I said. My fingers turned red and started to blister.

"*Shit*," Huon swore. "Summer!"

I dropped my pack to the ground and pulled out a water gourd. I undid the stopper with my teeth and poured water all over my hand. The second it touched, the pain stopped. A moment later the blistering was gone. In another half a dozen heartbeats, the skin on my fingers was healed as though nothing had happened.

"Well that was strange." I flexed my fingers. "Not even a hint of pain." I eyed the trees.

"Magic," Kale said simply. "I suspect if we didn't have magic, things might have been much worse." He nodded at me. "Yours healed you, and quickly." He looked impressed.

I chewed my lip and examined my hands up close to my face. Even the tinge of pink was gone. "Without lesser magic, the trees can't heal themselves. That doesn't explain why they smell like dead creatures, instead of trees."

"Maybe someone turned trolls into trees," Saff said. "Their touch can be toxic to Fae. Or so I've been told." He smiled lopsidedly.

I squinted. "They just look like trees to me." I had never heard that about trolls, but I refused to take his bait.

"That's what they would want you to think." He tapped the side of his nose.

"Unless someone can do a reversal spell, there's no way to know." I looked around the guys, but none of them said anything. I wasn't expecting them to. The ability to reverse spells was rare, and in the Fae realm it was considered rude. I mean, someone went to all that hassle to do magic, only to have someone come along and undo it? It was like walking with muddy feet on newly cleaned floors.

"We should walk from here," Huon said. "Conserve our strength."

"And see what other weird shit is going on," Saff added.

"That too," Huon agreed.

They started to move carefully around the trees. After a moment, and at a safe distance from the foliage, I followed.

Kale fell into step beside me.

"Have you ever seen anything like this?" I ducked around a pine with needles which glistened with unnatural moisture.

"Never," he replied. "I am, however, concerned about the rivers and lakes."

I tilted my head at him. "You are? Why?"

He glanced at me. "Whatever falls to the ground can fall into water, or be washed into it."

I frowned. "Stinking, stinging leaves could taint the water," I concluded.

"And anyone who drinks it," he agreed.

I thought about the water under the rose bower. That was fresh yesterday, but what about now? Or next week?

Or next year?

"It's not this bad near the capital." I adjusted my pack and stepped over a fallen log.

"Nor near Springblade," he said, "but if it gets worse the farther we are from Fae settlements..."

"It could be a lot worse than this," I finished for him. "Or maybe it's because we're closer to where the trolls live."

He looked to be considering that for a moment before he said, "That is possible. They do seem to spread taint wherever they go." After another moment he spoke again. "Did you know we're related?"

I frowned. "You and I?" A spike of disappointment blossomed in my chest. It died when he laughed softly.

"No. The Fae and trolls."

"Oh," I replied. "That's much worse."

He smiled, the first one I'd seen from him since we left the capital. "It's certainly not pleasant, but it's true."

"Of course, because we're snub nosed, short-legged, short-lived and nasty," I replied sarcastically.

"You're not that bad," Huon said from up ahead. He turned and gave me a grin.

I made a rude gesture with my finger and he laughed.

"You're right, that description matches Saff better." Huon ducked under Saff's arm as his friend swung at him playfully. "Hey, is that any way to treat your king?"

I locked eyes with Saff and we simultaneously said, "Yes!" and dissolved into laughter.

Kale shook his head at us. "I hope we're not trying to sneak up on any trolls. They would have heard us coming for days."

Huon blinked at him. "Did you just make a joke?"

"I didn't intend to," Kale replied, his brow creased slightly. "We *are* making a lot of noise."

"He's right, we sound like a herd of screamspinners." I shuddered. The ten-legged creatures spun enormous, sticky webs, then moved away to hide. When they spotted their prey, they screamed like a Fae having its wings pulled off. The sound scared their prey toward the webs, where they'd get stuck before they got eaten.

Slowly.

"They don't travel in herds," Saff pointed out.

"Be grateful for that," I said.

"They might mask any noise we make," Huon pointed out.

"Or we could be quiet," Kale suggested.

"That's the best idea I've heard all day," I said, my

voice low. "So tell me, how are we related to trolls?" I stepped around a beech with more rotten leaves than not. It stank like a dead pig's ass. Not that I had ever been near one, much less smelled it, but it was putrid nonetheless.

"We evolved from the same creature," Kale replied. "As did the screamspinners."

"That explains my sisters," I said cheerfully. "Part troll, part screamspinner."

"I'm sure they aren't that bad," he said.

"You clearly haven't met them." I sighed. "No, they aren't *that* bad, just irritating, judgemental, difficult, spoilt…" I held up a finger as Huon looked over his shoulder, his mouth open.

"Don't say a word," I warned.

He held up his hands and gave me a look of pure mock innocence. "I wouldn't dream of it."

"Of course not," Saff said, "you just described him to a T."

He ducked away from Huon and the ground fell out from under him.

CHAPTER SIX

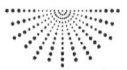

"What the hells?" Huon exclaimed.
I froze.

"Saff?" I called out gingerly.

"I'm all right, just a little bruised." His voice came back from a hole which had been covered by sticks and leaves. When he'd stepped in the wrong place, the camouflage had given way.

The trap was the oldest one in the book, here and in the human world. We probably should have been on the lookout for it, but my eyes were on the leaves nearest my face, not on the ground.

"You should probably come down here though," Saff added.

I exchanged confused looks with Huon, but slowly moved toward the hole.

"Why?" I asked. "What's down there?" If this was a joke of some kind, I would...

"Something amazing," Saff replied. "You have to see it for yourself."

I frowned, but inched forward before I peered over the edge.

Saff lay on his side, eyes closed, face white except for a smattering of blood on his cheek. Beside him sat a large creature with striped black and grey fur.

"A mimicat," I said. It hadn't been Saff speaking at all. The big cats were known for their ability to mimic voices perfectly.

And for their appetite.

The mimicat licked his paw.

"It looks as though I eat well tonight." Now the mimicat sounded like me.

"Not if we kill you first." Huon pulled out a knife.

"Kill me? Don't you know you should always be gentle with pussies?" The mimicat tilted his head.

"Not ones who are about to try to eat my friend," Huon growled.

"Why would I eat him?" the mimicat asked, now speaking in Huon's voice. "You look much tastier. Or her." The cat inclined his head toward me. "But I can make you a deal. I won't eat any of you." He flicked his tail.

"What do you want in return?" Kale asked.

"The same thing you want." The mimicat used a different voice now, maybe its own, maybe a past victim. "The return of lesser magic. Without the ability to cross the veil, we're dying out. Trolls are unpalatable and Fae are vengeful if we eat one of them. Don't even get me started on eating scream-spinners."

"You eat humans?" I asked, aghast.

The mimicat looked affronted. "Only the bad ones. Mostly we just eat rats and mice and the fish humans toss out for us."

"So if we get lesser magic back, you won't eat us?" Huon asked.

"Better than that, I want to help you." The mimicat stepped over to Saff and licked his face before anyone could object.

Saff gave a soft groan and started to rouse.

"We're not without magic of our own. I think we can assist each other. My name is Khatlintain. You can call me Khat if you prefer." He drew the name out, including the H.

Huon eyed him for a few moments longer, then slid his knife away. "Saff?"

Saff groaned and sat up. "I'm all right. Nothing hurt but my self-esteem."

"So, nothing vital then." Huon gave a wan smile.

"Pretty much." Saff pushed himself to his feet. "Why is a cat digging a hole and hiding in it?"

"That's Khat to you," Khat replied. "You have to say the H. K...h...h...hat."

Saff shrugged. "Like I said, cat."

"Maybe I will eat him after all," Khat said in my voice.

Saff peered up at us. "Is it wrong that I found that arousing?"

I turned to Kale. "Maybe we should leave him in the hole."

Kale nodded. "That might be wise." Humour shone in his eyes. "But he asked a pertinent question. Why did a mimicat dig a hole and cover it?"

"I didn't," Khat replied. "I found it and hid in it. We mimicats like dark places, you know. No one asked you to fall in and wake me from my nap." His ears and tail flicked back and forth now.

"Um, I don't mean to be rude—" I started.

"Then don't," Khat replied.

I hesitated for a moment, but then asked, "Are all mimicats as strange as you?"

Khat sniffed. "Of course we are." He blinked at me slowly. "You ask that as though being strange is a bad thing."

I laughed. The creature was odd, but it was hard not to like him.

Huon laughed louder than I did. "The cat has a point."

"Khat," said Khat.

"So how can you help us?" I asked. "Do you know what caused lesser magic to fail?"

"Alas, I don't," he said sadly. "I suspect the answer lies here, in the west. The rest of the mimicat council—"

"You have a council?" Huon blurted out.

"Of course we do." Khat sounded offended. "We're not uncivilised." His tail swished again.

I was starting to realise that was a sign of his aggravation.

"Of course you're not." I shot Huon a warning look. "We just don't know much about your kind."

"You could have learnt," Khat said.

"Since your kind eats our kind, I think we can be forgiven for not trying too hard," Huon said dryly. "Hopefully this can lead to a new era of peace between the mimicats and Fae."

"And a new era of mutually not eating each other," Saff added.

Khat stretched slowly and leapt out of the hole.

I stepped back. Next to me, he was twice my

current size. In the human world, he would be no bigger than a kitten. I resisted the urge to enlarge myself. We stayed small to reduce our impact on the realm around us. It would be irresponsible to do otherwise just for my own ego.

Huon looked as though he'd been thinking the same thing, but he too remained small.

"So," I said uneasily, "what did the council think?"

"They dealt with it the way they deal with everything. They decided to take a nap and worry about it later." He sounded disgusted. "There may or may not have been some idle ass-licking involved as well."

I grimaced.

"So why are you here?" Saff flew up out of the hole and landed beside me.

Khat's head swivelled to look at each of us in turn. "Why are any of you? You all care more than the rest of the Fae. Am I right? The rest are too busy being self important and indolent."

Huon raised a hand as though to argue, but lowered it again. "That, and the late king gave us the responsibility."

"Would you be here if he hadn't?"

"I would," I replied immediately.

"As would I," Kale replied.

"Me too," Saff said, eying me unashamedly.

"And you?" Khat asked Huon. "Or would you have sent them on your behalf, your highness?"

Huon's eyes widened. "How did you know?"

"I said I'm not without my magic," Khat replied. He blinked and slowly began to shrink down until he matched the rest of us in size. "So, would you be here?"

"I don't know," Huon admitted, "but that doesn't answer Saff's question."

"I'm a rebel," Khat replied. "Also I have a mate and kittens on the other side of the veil."

"A regular cat?" Saff asked.

"Good gracious no!" Khat replied, affronted. "She's a perfectly good mimicat, I'll have you know. She just started to give birth at the wrong time. I came back here for help and the veil closed. I've been stuck here ever since and she's been stuck there."

"That's terrible." I genuinely felt bad for him. "We're going to fix this. We have Fae on the other side too."

Huon nodded. "Khat, do you have any idea where to start on this? All we have is, 'somewhere in the west,' but the west is a big place. It's hundreds of kilometres from coast to coast, and mostly places Fae don't go. Or won't go."

"Too many trolls," Khat agreed. "And screamspinners. I heard rumours once of a cave full of them, and something of immense magical power at the other end."

"What sort of something?" Huon asked.

Khat sniffed. "I have no idea. No one I know who has gone there has ever come back."

"Well that doesn't sound like a bad idea at all," I said sarcastically.

I paused and looked around, then groaned. "We're going there, aren't we?"

"It could be the key," Huon said.

"Or a dead end," I pointed out.

"Literally," Saff added.

"I'm sure four Fae can overcome—" Huon began.

Khat cleared his throat.

"—four Fae and a mimicat," Huon corrected. "Can overcome a bunch of screamspinners."

"Or die trying," Saff said cheerfully.

"How do we know this isn't a trap?" Kale asked. "You might be trying to lure us to our death."

"I might be, but if I was, I would have eaten you already," Khat said. "What benefit would there be in sharing you all with screamspinners? Not to mention I prefer not to become their meal myself."

He sat down to scratch his neck. "I heard of a mimicat whom they took and devoured slowly. In the end, he could only scream like them before he died."

I shuddered. "In the human world, they use bug spray to kill insects and arachnids. Usually I wouldn't approve of the killing of any creature, but I'd feel better if we had a giant spray can we could bring with us."

Saff murmured his agreement.

"Let's worry about that when we get there." Huon said. "Khat did say it was just a rumour. How many times have we heard rumours that aren't true?"

"Once or twice," I agreed. "Khat, do you know the way to this cave that may or may not exist?"

"West, near the foot of the mountains," Khat replied.

"Well, that narrows it down a little." I sighed. The Border Mountains spanned at least a hundred kilometres.

"It's as good a place as any to start," Saff said cheerfully.

"Yes, and we will not get there if we stand here talking about it," Khat pointed out.

"The cat is right." Saff jerked a thumb toward him. "Lead on then."

"Me?" Khat asked. "Oh no, I don't lead. I said I would help."

"Scared the screampinners will get your first?" Huon asked teasingly.

"Precisely. I may look cute and furry, but I'm not an idiot. No, I will tag along behind you."

"If any trolls are following, they'll get him first," I said helpfully.

Khat paused. "As I said, I'll travel in the middle."

"I'll walk last," Kale said. "I can take care of myself."

Huon nodded. "Let's all stay close and keep an eye out for any more traps." He gave Saff a smirk.

"Hey, it was hidden," Saff argued. "It could just as easily have been you who fell in."

I shook my head and walked behind Khat as we made our way through the ever darkening trees.

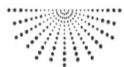

CHAPTER SEVEN

"*I*t seems clean," Huon reported.

I crouched beside him and drew a cupped hand of water from the wide lake. I sniffed at it carefully, then took a tiny sip. "It tastes all right."

Huon slurped the water in his own hand and nodded. "We can camp here for the night."

Grateful, I swung my pack down to the ground and rubbed my shoulders.

Huon gave me a look as though to offer to do it for me, but I stepped away from him. I felt his eyes on me, but I didn't look back. If I gave him a centimetre, he'd think he could take all of his centimetres and pound them into my pussy. I wasn't ready to forgive him, much less fuck him.

Along the edge of the lake, the trees looked

untouched by the taint. Their healthy green looked odd after several hours of brown.

"Is it possible the water contains something which is keeping them from rotting?" I asked Kale as he stopped beside me to regard the foliage more closely. "A bit of lesser magic maybe?"

"It's possible," he agreed. "Trees and plants which grow beside water are often stronger and more healthy because they have a source of water so close."

"That's true," I agreed. "Do you think it's safe to swim in?"

"I expect so. If it's fresh enough to drink, it should be clean enough to bathe."

I eyed the water. A fish darted across the surface and disappeared under a lily pad on the far side of the lake.

"Well, if it's good enough for the fish..." I followed the lake around to a stand of weeping willows and stripped. I tucked my clothes into a gap between two tree roots, where they should stay dry.

The water was cold on my bare feet. I stopped and waited a few moments for my skin to become accustomed, then waded in a little further. When the water was waist-deep, I paused.

A whoop of joy and a splash broke the silence as Saff leapt out off a thick branch. Legs tucked up, arms wound around them, he landed in the lake like a rock.

A wave washed over me, up to my chest. I squealed at the sudden cold on my breasts. I pressed my arms across them and ducked down until the water was up to my neck.

"You're a brat," I said once he surfaced for air.

He grinned. His eyes widened and he threw his hands over his face as Huon slammed into the water beside him.

A wash of water drenched my face and hair. I spat out a mouthful.

"And you called *me* a brat." Saff laughed. He scooped a handful of water and flung it at Huon as he popped up and took a breath.

Huon returned the favour, then splashed me for good measure.

"This means war," Saff said with a grin. He flicked the water with both hands, driving it relentlessly toward Huon's face.

Huon splashed him back. He moved closer to Saff, a bounce with each step.

I shook my head and picked a side. I lay back, stretched out my legs and kicked in Huon's direction.

"Hey, I thought we were friends?" he protested.

"What made you think that?" I kept up my attack, while I paddled with my arms to stay in place.

"You're vicious for a Fae," he teased. In spite of the onslaught, he grabbed my ankle and yanked me toward him.

I let out a shriek and tried to slip free from his grasp.

He managed to grip onto my other ankle and pulled until my legs went around his hips.

I tried to paddle backward, but he got his hands on my waist and drew me closer so my stomach was touching his cock.

"I'm mad at you," I reminded him.

"I'm sorry," he replied. "I shouldn't have talked about you behind your back. I just find it hard not to talk about you. Or touch you." His hands slid up and down my sides.

"You told Saff you would share me, with no thought to my feelings." My tone was colder than I'd intended, but I need to make this point. My life was *my* choice to make, no one else's.

Unless you count Birch having sent us on this quest to start with.

Huon surprised me by laughing.

"As if anyone could ever tell you how to feel or act, or anything like that. Summer, you're the most independent Fae I know. All I said to Saff was that if you preferred him to me, I would have to accept it and live with it." He searched my eyes with his. "For all I know, you might have loathed him like you loathe me."

I sighed softly. "I don't loathe you, Huon. You drive me crazy, and sometimes you're a dick. You're immature, spoilt, selfish, difficult—"

"Wow, it sounds like loathe is an understatement."

He actually looked hurt.

I added more, to put him out of his misery.

"You're also smart, funny and I think you'll make a great king. Well, someday." I smiled teasingly.

He snorted. "No pressure then." Judging by how his erection now pressed against my stomach, there certainly *was* pressure.

"What about me?"

I had forgotten about Saff until he spoke over my shoulder.

I looked back at him. "You're goofy, funny and have that amazing hair." Right now it was plastered to his head and dripping down his face.

He grinned.

"You're pretty cute yourself," he said.

"Of course I am," I joked.

"So—" Huon ventured. "You don't hate us?"

I shook my head, sending droplets flying. "I don't hate either of you. I like you. Both of you. And Kale..." I added slowly.

"Ahhh." Huon nodded. "Well, Kale is pretty great."

"Really great," Saff agreed. "Smart and kind of hot."

I arched an eyebrow at Saff.

He shrugged. "I'm attracted to men and women. Is that a problem?"

"Not for me," I replied.

"Now we've worked that out..." Huon moved me up his body until the tip of his cock teased my pussy. He eased a fingertip inside me. "I'm going to fuck you."

I smiled and rubbed myself against him, driving him deeper.

"Um, should I go?" Saff asked.

It was sweet of him to ask, instead of making assumptions.

"I think you should stay," I said, my voice husky with growing desire.

In reply, he gently massaged my shoulders, then slipped a hand down and around to cup my breast. With his other hand, he grazed my pussy. He must have touched Huon's cock as well, because we both groaned.

Saff found my clit and gently ran his fingertip in tiny circles, while Huon slid himself all the way inside me.

Huon paused to exhale, then slid out again, all the way. Just as I was about to beg him to fill me again, he did.

Behind me, Saff's cock rested against my ass. With one hand, I reached around to grip his wet, hard length. He bucked into my fingers as I rocked against his.

Huon thrust, firm and confident, like he knew I'd forgive him. Waves splashed as he slid in and out of me, slapping back and forth between us.

Saff palmed one nipple, in rhythm with his movement, as Huon rolled the other gently.

Between all the stimulation and both men pressed in close, I was on fire in a handful of heartbeats. I closed my eyes and rolled my hips, rubbing myself faster against Saff's fingers.

"Oh gods," I breathed. "I'm going to—

"Not yet," Huon growled. "Don't let her come until she begs for it."

"You suck," I growled.

He chuckled. "You love it. Now beg. Beg for Saff to let you come."

I groaned. "Please. Please Saff..." I rocked against

him harder, barely able to stop myself from pitching over the edge.

"Please what?" Saff drew my hair aside and kissed my neck.

I didn't have words to tell him he also sucked. "Please let me come," I panted.

He hummed. "Okay, come for me, beautiful."

I couldn't have held back a moment longer anyway, but his words threw me over the cliff, hard and glittering with fireworks and distant universes exploding into dust.

"Do I have to beg too?" Saff asked, his voice muffled by the roar of blood in my ears.

"Hells yeah, you do," Huon agreed. He didn't even slow his even strokes into my body.

"Please, your highness, can I come?" Saff asked, breathing ragged.

"Yes, you may," Huon said graciously.

Saff came, thrusting harder into my curled fingers until the warmth of his cum squirted out into the water of the lake.

Huon followed a few moments later, grunting and thrusting. One hand gripped my hip, the other held my breast so hard it hurt. He pinched my nipple until I almost screamed. He stilled and spilled his cum inside me while he twisted my nipple.

Finally, he gasped and sagged, panting.

He slipped out of me and both men moved in closer to hold me while my heart slowed to a normal pace.

"Well, that was nice," Saff remarked.

Huon chuckled softly. "Very nice," he agreed. "I'm glad we had this little talk."

I smirked and socked him on the arm, sending a spray of water at his face. "You're such a pain in the ass."

He grinned. "That's all part of my charm."

I socked him again, then wriggled free of them both and swam a couple of metres away.

"Well, if the water was safe to drink, it no longer is," Khat remarked. He sat on the lakeshore, licking his paw.

I blushed slightly. "I'm sure it's still fine."

He lowered his paw to the ground and blinked at us. "Excuse me if I don't. Now, if you're done fucking, I think I've found something."

CHAPTER EIGHT

"*A* trapdoor?"

The mimicat had led us through a break in the trees, to a copse.

Here, the grass lay in patches; green here, brown there. It reminded me of a chessboard, but not so uniform. That was fortunate, I felt like enough of a pawn as it was.

The door lay in almost the dead centre of the copse. A ring of green grass surrounded it like a target.

"You know they're called trapdoors for a reason right?" Saff remarked.

"Because it's a trap?" Huon suggested.

"It's not much of one," Kale reasoned. "No

sensible Fae would miss it, sitting here in the open as it is."

"Sensible being the keyword here," I muttered. "I don't think even a troll would be stupid enough to go down there."

Silence fell.

"You're going to suggest we open it, aren't you?" Saff looked toward Huon.

Huon tapped his fingers against his lips. "We could stand here and speculate all day about what might be in there, or we could just open it."

"After you." I stepped back, my hands raised to ward off anything which might leap out.

"You're usually the first one to jump into potential trouble," Huon said.

"Do I need to remind you it's called a *trapdoor?*" I planted my hands on my hips. "It could be full of screamspinners." I shuddered.

"Or worse," Saff agreed.

I turned to him, eyes wide. "Worse? What could possibly be worse?"

He shrugged. "Fae-eating snails?"

I blinked. "I beg your pardon?"

"Fae-eating snails," he repeated. "You know, snails that eat—"

"Yes, I guessed what they might eat," I replied

hotly. "Don't tell me, they do it really slowly, so their food suffers, while covered in slimy goo?"

He grinned. "Sounds about right."

"I don't think there is such a thing," Kale said slowly. "However, you should all stand back. I will open the door."

"Why you?" Huon asked.

"Summer prefers not to," Kale replied. "You are king and shouldn't put yourself in harm's way more than necessary. Khat has no hands."

"Yes, thank you for the reminder," Khat said sarcastically.

"What about me?" Saff asked.

Kale turned his dark-eyed gaze toward Saff. "Because you might fall in."

Saff raised a finger as if to argue, then lowered it. "Good point. Safe distance it is."

We all stepped back and Kale crouched beside the door. He pushed back the grass that grew around the edges.

He spoke as he worked. "There's a lock. It's rusty." He tugged at it. "It's still good enough not to disintegrate on touch. I'll use a little magic."

The lock clicked and he removed it and placed it aside.

"All right, now for the door." He grabbed onto the

handle—a plain circle of steel—and tugged.

In spite of the potential danger of the situation, I couldn't help but admire his muscles and the way they bulged as he strained. From the choking sound coming from Saff's direction, he noticed as well.

"Do you need some help?" Saff asked, his voice higher than usual.

I bit back a snort and glanced toward Huon. He wore a slight smile on his face, but looked impatient. I knew him well enough to know he too wanted to step in and help. Standing back to watch had never been his thing. Well, not in this type of situation.

Kale looked up at Saff, a thoughtful expression on his face. "Perhaps you could take hold of the end and give it a tug."

Saff swallowed audibly. "I can do that," he squeaked. He cleared his throat and got a grip on the other side of the door. He bent his legs and heaved. His face turned as red as his hair with the exertion.

"Is it heavy, or stuck?" I peered around Saff's shoulder. I couldn't spot anything that would serve as an impediment to the door opening. I assumed it must be more solid than it looked, until Kale let the handle go and sat back.

"I think it's fastened shut with magic."

"Well, that seals that then," Saff said. When we all

turned to look at him and groan, he added, "No pun intended."

"*Sure* it wasn't." I pulled a face at him, which he responded to by sticking out his tongue and wiggling it.

"I'm surrounded by children," Khat said sadly.

"I know the feeling." I gave a mock heavy sigh.

Khat flicked his tail back and forth, then addressed me in my own voice. "You Fae are such a lot of frivolous flittabouts, I don't know how you haven't all gone extinct. Oh yes, screwing in lakes."

I raised my eyebrows. "I've never said the word flittabout in my life."

"You just did," Huon pointed out.

"Says the king of frivolous flittabouts," I said. "Literally and figuratively."

"I rest my case." Khat exhaled heavily, flopped down and rested his head on his front paws. "If I had hands, I wouldn't need your help."

"Well, here you are." Huon shook his head. "Fighting amongst ourselves isn't going to help anyone."

"That's the first sensible thing anyone has said since we met," Khat said.

"Kale and Summer have both said plenty of sensible things," Saff said helpfully.

"Exactly." I nodded. "Now, are we going to use magic to open this door, or are we going to take the hint and leave it the hells alone?" What were the chances it had anything to do with lesser magic anyway?

It might just be a door.

In the middle of a copse.

Deep in the forest.

Leading nowhere in particular.

I rubbed my forehead. "We're using magic on this thing, aren't we?"

"Yes." Huon nodded. "Yes we are. You can stand further back if you like."

I thought for a moment. "I don't know. Blasting the shit out of things is one of my talents, remember?"

"This is not a rose petal," Kale pointed out.

"It's just wood." I stepped closer and eyed it.

"Wood and magic. Higher magic." Kale rose to his feet. "Tampering with it could cause blowback."

Saff opened his mouth, but closed it again when I gave him a look.

"Not everything is about sex," I said.

He blinked and was silent for a moment. Then he said, "Yes it is, if you think about it hard enough. Again, no pun intended."

"I don't agree." I tilted my head and tried not to smile. "I think that pun *was* intended."

"I tend to concur," Huon said with a mirthful nod. "He definitely meant it."

Saff gave us a cheeky eyebrow wiggle and shrugged. "My point stands." He looked surprised, then grinned. "Now *that*, I really didn't mean."

I shook my head. "Meanwhile, we have a door to open." I looked down at it and frowned. "Would now be a good time to remind you I think this is a really bad idea? I mean, who would leave a door just lying around here?"

"Pre-Fae civilisation?" Saff suggested.

I couldn't tell if he was joking or not. "I don't think a door would last long enough to outlive a single Fae, much less predate any of us."

"Unless magic was involved," Huon reasoned. "Which it clearly is."

"The king is correct," Kale said. "The right magic could preserve an artefact far beyond its usual limits. It's possible this very spot has something to do with the loss of lesser magic."

"But Khat said it involved a cave in the mountains, and a bunch of screamspinners." I gestured toward the mimicat.

"I also said it was a theory," Khat said. He

scratched his ear with a back paw. "While I also don't think opening the trapdoor is a good idea, we're here now. If nothing comes of this, we can continue toward the mountains."

"Unless we die here," Saff said helpfully. "In which case, we won't be going anywhere after this."

"Thank you for that observation," I said dryly. "This is where someone suggests we split up, isn't it? Two of us stay here and three go on, or some such?"

"No." Huon shook his head. "Whatever happens, we stay together. All of us." He looked at us, one after the other, even Khat. "We're stronger in a group, with all of our magic. And for the record," he fixed Saff with a frown, "none of us are going to die any time soon."

"Ahhh, you're a seer," Khat remarked.

Huon scowled at him. "No, I'm an optimist."

"A seer would be more useful," Khat said.

"I'm sure it would, but I can't help that," Huon said curtly.

"Evidently." Khat's ears twitched.

"I hope you have something more useful to contribute than a few snide remarks." Huon narrowed his eyes at the mimicat. "Because we have Summer for that." He waved toward me.

"I'm not sure if I should say thank you or be offended," I remarked.

"See?" Huon said. He flashed a smile at me. "You can thank me later."

I rolled my eyes. Fed up of all the chatter, I stepped over to the door.

"What is that?" I squinted.

"What is what?" Kale asked.

I pointed. "There's a symbol of some kind on the middle of the door." I stepped lightly onto it for a better look.

"That looks like a rose." I touched it lightly.

Light flashed and the world disappeared.

CHAPTER NINE

S hit.

Somewhere off to the right, water dripped. At least, I hoped it was water.

I sniffed. I couldn't smell anything worse than dank and stale air.

Gradually, my eyes got used to the dark. A sliver of light from up above my head penetrated the gloom. It wasn't much in the way of illumination, but at least it wasn't pitch dark in here.

Wherever in the hells *here* was.

"Is anyone there?" I called out softly.

My voice echoed back at me, twice as loud and lower pitched.

If I didn't know better...

"Who's there?" I took a tentative step forward.

The ground beneath my feet was hard, but smooth. Stone, but not natural stone. I felt out in front of me with the toe of my boot and found a straight join.

Paving of some kind. Not a cave then. That didn't mean I wasn't surrounded by screamspinners.

"Who's there?" a voice asked. It copied my tone, but it was definitely *not* an echo.

"I asked first," I replied. Before the voice could respond, I raised my hand and magiced up a little light.

The voice hissed. A shape, easily as big as me, scurried into the shadows. I caught a glimpse of eyes before an arm was thrown up to cover it.

"Too bright!" The voice was hoarse, but undeniably male.

"Um, sorry, let me turn it down." I closed my hand and reduced the amount of magic in the spell. "Is that better?"

The shape lowered his arm. Most of his face was obscured by a hood, but his eyes shone in the dim light. They looked huge, as though he spent all of his time in the dark. Given where we were, it wasn't much of a stretch to assume he had.

"Who are you?" I asked.

"Remington," he replied. "Fletcher Remington."

"That's not a Fae name," I remarked.

"No, it's not," he agreed. He pushed his hood back.

I stared for a moment. "Oh, sweet fucked up gods, you're human!" Shrunk down to the same size as me, but human nonetheless.

He gave me an awkward bow, his hand pressed to his chest. "Indeed I am. And you are…"

"Summer," I supplied.

"That's not a Fae name either," he pointed out.

I snorted. "Don't you start."

"I beg your pardon?"

I waved my hand, making the light dance across the floor. "It doesn't matter. Where is this place and what are you doing here?"

"I stopped counting how long I've been here after the first year," he said, "and I still can't answer the question of where this is. As for how—" he shrugged. "Probably the same way you did."

"The trapdoor that lived up to its name." I sighed.

He nodded. "It seems to be a portal to here. Without light, I haven't been able to explore too far. Just enough to find a pool to drink from, and mushrooms to eat."

"Just mushrooms?"

"Yes." He rubbed his bearded chin. "I don't suppose you brought a hamburger?"

"A what?" I asked. "Oh, that meat thing humans eat in the human realm?"

"I'd make do with pizza," he added.

"I have bread and cheese," I said, "but there's more of that when we get out of here." There had to be a way out. I hoped Huon had the sense to keep himself, or any of the guys from following me.

I waited. None of them appeared.

"I don't suppose you know how far we are from the trapdoor?" I asked.

Before he could answer, I raised my hand toward the ceiling. The faint light source was a crack in the stone, a neat, even line.

No sign of the trapdoor.

"I don't know," Fletcher replied. "I haven't seen it since I've been here."

"I'm guessing you don't know where *here* is?"

"Not a clue," he replied. "If I had to speculate, I'd say we're in the mountains. The floors are paved, but the walls are just stone."

He was right. I ran my hand across one. The surface was rough, but even, as if someone had carved a passageway through the rock.

"No point calling for help then," I mused. "There are other tunnels leading from here?"

"Yes." He nodded. "One going that way, up toward

the water and mushrooms. Another goes down the other way. I only made it a short distance before I fell down some stairs. After that I came back and stayed around here."

"So we pick a direction and head that way." I rubbed my forehead. "If we're in the mountains, then down is the way we need to go to get out."

"In theory," he agreed.

I frowned at him. "You don't agree? What is a human doing in a cave in the Fae realm anyway?"

He hesitated before answering. "A friend brought me. When the veil shut between worlds, I was stuck in this realm. I decided to explore."

"And then you got stuck here. Is getting stuck in places something you make a habit of?"

He snorted. "It's usually something I avoid, if I can help it. Apparently magic happens."

"That it does," I agreed. "All right then. Unless you have a better idea, we're going down."

Silence fell for a moment.

Fletcher cleared his throat. "Is something wrong?"

"No. I was waiting for a friend of mine to make a joke. Then I remembered he's still out there." Assuming Saff was still near the trapdoor.

"Ahhh. I can make a joke if it will make you feel more comfortable," Fletcher offered.

"Would you?" I was feeling disconcerted by the whole situation. I didn't mind the dark, but this much of it was oppressive. Without Huon, Saff, Kale and even Khat, I was more than a little bit lost.

"Um, sure. Let me see... Going down sounds like a great idea." He sighed. "Sorry, I'm out of practice with innuendos. I haven't had anyone to talk to for so long."

I gave him a pat on the arm. "You did fine. I appreciate the effort anyway."

"I'll try harder next time."

"Not too hard though," I said. "If you try too hard, it won't be funny."

"I'll bear that in mind, thank you."

"You're welcome. Now, do you have a bag or anything, or can we get going?"

"I carry everything I have in my pockets," he replied.

"All right then, let's go." I raised my hand toward the tunnel and started walking. "How far down were the stairs?"

"Not far, but it's hard to tell. I was going slowly, taking my time in the dark."

"It's good to go slowly sometimes," I agreed.

"You're much better at innuendos than I am," he said.

I laughed, but stopped when it echoed back at me.

"I think I see stairs up ahead." I lowered my hand and peered into the gloom. The tunnel disappeared down into further darkness. "How did you not go crazy in all this darkness?"

He laughed bitterly. "Who said I haven't?"

"You seem pretty sane to me," I replied. "You don't even smell bad."

"I washed in the underground pool back there," he said. "Thanks for noticing. I figured I should keep clean in case I got a visitor some day."

"That's very thoughtful of you," I told him.

"Thanks," he said again. "I figured someone would come and bring light. And here you are."

"Why did you figure that?" I stepped to the top of the stairs and peered downward. I couldn't see the bottom, but there had to be one.

"Because I haven't found any bones here."

I stopped dead. "What did you say?"

He repeated himself. "Why? Is that a bad thing?"

"I might mean people got out," I said slowly, "and it might mean something ate the bones."

"Something?" he echoed. "I don't want anything to eat my bones. Well, apart from a pretty girl."

In spite of my growing fear, I smiled. "See, that was a good one."

"You can't see me, but I'm blushing. Now, do I want to know what in the Fae realm might eat bones?"

I shrugged. "Probably not." I stepped down the stairs, one at a time.

Fletcher stayed close behind, almost close enough to breathe on the back of my neck.

"I see why you fell down these," I remarked. Spaced at irregular intervals, each step was uneven and slick. From what, I couldn't tell. Maybe the water in the pool Fletcher mentioned trickled down here a little bit too.

"My father was a builder," Fletcher said. "He wouldn't have approved of the quality of the work either."

The stairs wound around gradually as we descended. They also became increasingly narrow, until the space was so close I almost touched each wall with my elbows.

"We must be almost to the end of the stairs—oh." I stepped around a bend and almost walked into a door.

At the last moment I caught myself and skidded to a stop.

I shone my magic onto it. In the dead centre of the door was the same symbol on the trapdoor, a rose encircled with a series of knots.

"Oh hells no," I said. "I am not falling for that again. No way." I backed up a few steps. "We'll need to go back and try the other way."

"It's a dead end." He worked his way past me and peered at the symbol. "Can you shine a light on the door?"

Reluctantly, I obliged. "I'd rather be as far away from this as I can get," I said.

"It's a keyhole," he said.

I frowned. "What?"

He gestured toward the symbol. "There's a keyhole beside the symbol."

"So?"

He blinked. "I don't know. I suppose it must lead somewhere if we could open it."

"Do you happen to have a key in your pocket?" I asked.

"Only the ones to my house and car," he replied. "My plants are probably dead by now." He rubbed his beard. "Maybe people are the key. People or Fae," he added quickly. "That's why we ended up here and no one else did."

"Or maybe someone decided to fuck with anyone who got stuck here." I lowered my hand and crossed my arms.

"I suppose that's possible as well," he conceded. "Should we try to open it?"

"We tried that with the trapdoor and look where that got us." I told him about Kale trying to tug it open. "I assume you tried the same thing?"

"I did," he agreed. "There was no visible lock on it though."

"We still ended up here." I tapped my fingers against my chin. "I've read extensively and I've never seen or heard of a symbol like that, much less one which transports Fae, or people, to places like this."

"I might regret this, but I'm going to touch the symbol." He raised his hand toward it.

I caught his wrist. "No you're not."

"One of us has to," Fletcher argued. "If you keep holding on to me, you'll be transported too."

Reluctantly, I let go and stepped back. "This is crazy."

"It might be crazy. It might also explain why there are no bones here. Anyone who has come here before has left." He cocked his head at me. "It's worth a try."

I shrugged and waved a hand toward the door. I had heard that tone too many times from Birch and Huon. And, if I was honest, myself. When I was determined to do something, I did it, no matter what anyone else said.

"Go ahead," I said.

He turned his back and reached out. His fingertips brushed the symbol.

I held my breath.

Nothing happened.

"Hmmm, did you put a hand on the one on the trapdoor?" he asked.

"No." I shook my head. "I just got near it. Before you ask, I'm not going any closer."

"But what if—"

"No," I said firmly. "I want to get out of here, but not if we end up somewhere worse." I thought for a moment. "I have an idea, but you might not like it?"

"Does it end in a hamburger?"

"Um, sure, why not." If he liked them made from vegetables, since Fae didn't eat meat.

"Then I'm in. What is this idea?"

I told him.

"I said you might not like it."

CHAPTER TEN

"*I* hate small spaces," Fletcher remarked.

"You've been stuck in the dark for how long?" I glanced over at him.

"Long enough to hate small spaces," he replied. After a moment, he added, "It depends on the space though."

"Four," I said.

"Four what?" he asked.

"On a scale of one to ten, I rate that innuendo a four."

"Oh, you're keeping score now?" He sounded amused, but my light was directed at the stairs as we ascended them.

"I wasn't, but I could." I smiled.

He laughed. "What would it take to get a ten?"

I thought for a moment. "I don't know. I suppose you'll find out when you get there." I found myself liking him. His voice was a warm, deep rumble and he obviously had a sense of humour. Apart from having a beard, which would be a side effect of being stuck in here, I had no idea what he looked like.

I liked to think I wasn't shallow, but Huon, Saff and Kale were all hot guys. Thinking about them made my heart skip and ache. I wanted to see all of them, and I would, if I ever get out of here.

And I could satisfy my growing curiosity about what Fletcher looked like.

I imagined him having dark hair and maybe dark brown eyes, like chocolate. He probably had perfect teeth and soft warm lips I could—

I swallowed hard. Now was *not* the time to be thinking like this.

"I'll keep trying then," he assured me.

We stepped in the same place I'd arrived and looked around on the ground.

"Is something wrong?" he asked.

"No, I was just wondering if that symbol was on the floor somewhere. I wouldn't want to accidentally step on it."

Fletcher grabbed my hand. His was firm and

rough with callouses. His fingers curled around mine. "Just in case one of us is transported out of here," he explained. "At least this way we'll go together."

"Either way, we will." I looked up toward the crack in the ceiling. "I assume, since you're here, you're familiar with the Fae ability to make things smaller?"

"I am."

His hand trembled.

"All right then. Hold on tight." I squeezed his hand.

Before I was able to do anything, he said, "Wait!"

I froze. "What? Is something wrong?"

"Just an idea, but what if, instead of shrinking, we grow so big we bust ourselves out of here?" he said.

"What if the walls don't move and we break every bone in our bodies?" I replied.

"Is that possible?"

"So I've heard. Don't worry, we can do this, all right? Trust me."

"I hate those words," he muttered. "They usually come before something bad."

"Not this time," I assured him. "Now hold on." I licked my lips and let my magic work on us both.

At first, it seemed like nothing happened. Then

the crack in the ceiling grew further and further away. I didn't dare to take a step. Having reduced us both in size so drastically, we risked falling into a gap between the paving stones.

"All right, put your arms around me. I'll fly us out of here."

He didn't let my hand go until he had one arm tight around my waist. Then, like he was scared I might zip away without warning, he quickly grabbed on with the other.

"Maybe not so tight; I can't breathe," I suggested.

"Oh, sorry." He loosened his grip slightly. "Flying isn't my favourite thing to do."

"It is mine." I put an arm around him and jumped off the ground, wings flapping hard to drive us up toward the ceiling.

Manoeuvring with his weight added to mine was clumsy, and the going was slower than usual, but we neared the crack after a minute or two. Being smaller, we could have been flying all the way to the sky it felt so far. Whatever got us out of here.

"Are you sure we'll fit in there?" he asked, his voice raised against the rush of wind.

"We'll have to, won't we?" I replied. "Keep your hands and feet tucked close to me."

"Shit," he muttered.

I drew my wings in a little and flitted into the crack. To be honest I wasn't sure if we would make it. I ducked my head to avoid a piece of broken stone that looked sharp enough to slice off a layer or two of skin.

The crack itself went deeper than I thought. The light got brighter, but on and on it went.

Finally, I began to tire and was forced to land in a tiny nook in the stone. At normal size, it might have fit my fingertip. At our current size, we had enough space to step apart and breathe.

"Don't get too close to the edge," I suggested. "It's a long way down."

I didn't have to worry. Fletcher sat down and pressed himself against the wall. The hood fell over the sides of his face.

"Are you all right?" I crouched down in front of him. I still couldn't make out much of his features, even when he looked up at me.

"Yes. No." He sighed.

"It's all right if you're not," I said gently. "You were down there for a long time."

"Technically I still am," he pointed out, "but I'm worried about what happens afterward. What if I've gone crazy and I don't know it yet?"

I frowned. "I think you might know if you had."

"Would I? Maybe you're a figment of my imagination."

I pinched him hard on the arm.

"Ouch." He jerked his arm away. "Okay, you might be real."

"I feel as though I might be," I agreed. "Maybe we can rest here for a while and have something to eat." I pulled my bag off my back and drew out some bread and cheese. I offered them both to him.

"Do you want some too?" He sounded so ravenous, I pushed my own hunger aside and shook my head.

"No, it's fine. Go ahead and eat."

He unwrapped the bread, broke a bit off and stuffed it into his mouth. He moaned. "Crap, I'd forgotten how good bread tastes." I could barely make out the words with his mouth so full, but that was the gist.

I smiled softly. "Now I wish I had some cake."

"No cake? "he asked through a mouthful.

"Not even a crumb," I said sadly. "Although if I had, I would have eaten it already."

"I don't blame you. I miss cake."

"You probably miss a lot of things," I said carefully. "Apart from your houseplants. Do you have a girlfriend in the human realm? Or a boyfriend?"

He snorted softly. "No. Neither of those. Just my plants and my work. Then again, I've probably been fired by now."

For some reason, I was pleased he didn't have a girlfriend. Not that I didn't have my hands full with Huon, Saff and whatever I felt for Kale, but I was drawn to Fletcher as well.

"Your family must be worried." I moved to sit beside him.

"I only have a brother left, and he's probably thrilled to have the house to himself."

"You live together?"

"Yes. We inherited the house from our parents. It made sense to move in. At least, at the time."

"There's hope for those plants yet then," I said cheerfully.

He laughed around a chunk of cheese. "Naw, Rick wouldn't have bothered with them. He's too busy enjoying himself and his inheritance. Mine too by now, I suppose. Not that I care about money."

I visited the human realm often enough to know about money, but it seemed like an odd way to do things. We Fae worked in return for food and other things. Everyone had their skills and were happy— for the most part—to share.

"Money can buy cake, if I understand how money works," I said.

He laughed, low and bordering on bitter. "And chocolate. And coffee. I miss coffee even more than I miss hamburgers."

"Ah, coffee," I agreed. "We tried bringing it to the Fae realm, but for some reason it won't grow here."

"That sucks," he said.

"Agreed. It's another good reason to open the veil again." I peered out the mouth of our cozy little cave. "It's getting dark out there. Maybe we should stay here for the night. I don't want to risk getting lost in a crack in the stone."

He shifted beside me. "Neither do I, but I don't relish the idea of being here any longer than we have to either."

I put a hand on his and squeezed. "I know. We *will* get out of here." Even if we reached daylight in the morning, I still had no idea where *here* was. Hopefully tomorrow we'd find some answers.

"What's that?" he asked suddenly.

"What's what?"

"Shhh," he urged.

I did as he asked and listened.

A faint buzzing grew louder as whatever made the noise got closer and closer.

"Shit," I swore.

"Why? What is it?" he sounded frantic.

"I'm not sure, but I think we're about to find out why there are no bones here."

CHAPTER ELEVEN

I pressed myself against Fletcher as hard as I could and he did the same with me. Maybe by making ourselves look smaller, we might avoid being seen. I didn't say so, but I suspected us being seen might be the least of our concerns.

Sight was only one of the senses.

The buzzing got louder, echoing until I was forced to press my hands down over my ears to block out some of the noise.

A shadow dropped slowly past our little nook, then another. I made out wings and wide bodies.

"They look like beetles," Fletcher whispered into my ear.

I nodded and swallowed. "Blood beetles," I whispered back.

He groaned softly. "That sounds bad."

I nodded, but I had no more words, nothing of reassurance. At normal size, blood beetles were like leeches, or mosquitoes. They attached themselves to an unsuspecting Fae and sucked their blood, leaving them itchy and irritated.

At our present size, I had no idea what they might do. Honestly, I preferred not to find out.

Another beetle flew by, but then it popped back up. Mandibles chittered in our direction.

Shit.

Another beetle joined the first.

Then another.

"Maybe I could distract them while you fly away?" Fletcher suggested.

I glanced at him. "I'm not leaving you here."

"It's the sensible thing—"

I tried to laugh, but it came out as a grunt. Huon would have fallen over from laughing so hard if he knew anyone suggested I do something sensible.

All right, it happened from time to time, and perhaps it was the only way we could both escape, but I wasn't leaving an innocent human to his death.

No one deserved to die without eating cake one last time.

"The distraction is a good idea." I slowly rose to my feet. "Can you shout at them or something?"

A fourth beetle joined the others.

And fifth.

Fletcher sprang to his feet and waved his hands in the air.

"Hey, ugly bugs, over here. You're after a tasty tidbit? Look no further. Yoo-hoo, over here?"

Yoo-hoo?

Whatever, it worked.

I took a breath. *All right bitches, time to make like a petal.*

I lashed out with my magic.

The first beetle was knocked back against the others. It buzzed in irritation and shook its head. It seemed annoyed but undeterred. If anything, it moved faster toward us.

Shit.

"You're much less exploded than I hoped," I told it.

Fletcher kicked out at one of the beetles. He must have hit just the right spot, because it flew backward. It slammed into one of its companions and sent them both tumbling over the edge.

"Hell yeah!" He kicked at another but this one

stepped out of reach. "They have hard shells," he called out to me. "Can magic get past them?"

I clicked my fingers. "You're right." I dropped into a crouch and sent a blast of magic at the nearest beetle. This time I aimed under its mandibles.

The beetle wobbled for a moment, then blew apart. Chunks of beetle and shell flew in every direction.

"Fuck yeah." I threw my arm up over my face, then attacked another one.

This one blew apart like the first, but a large piece of shell flew toward Fletcher. It struck him hard in the shoulder and side of his head.

He grunted and slumped against the wall before sliding to the ground.

"Fletcher!"

A beetle headed straight for him, apparently thinking him an easier target than me. It got a finger-span away before my magic blasted the shit out of it.

The remaining beetle, which had stayed in the entry to the nook, now backed out and disappeared down the crack.

I waited, but the buzzing retreated until I could no longer hear it. I sagged in relief, breathing heavily, then stepped over toward Fletcher.

I slipped on a pile of beetle guts and had to wind-mill my arms and throw my wings out to avoid falling. Very graceful.

"Yuck." When we got out of here, I would have to wash my boots.

I added my knees to the list of things which needed bathing as I knelt next to Fletcher. The ground beside him was slick and littered with shards of shell.

"Fletcher?" I pressed my hand lightly to his chest. It rose and fell under my palm. Thank the gods, he was still alive.

I touched his head gingerly and felt a little blood and a growing bump, but nothing which seemed too serious.

He groaned. His head twitched.

"What the—"

"Don't move too much. You got knocked out by a piece of shell. You might have a bit of a headache, but I think you'll live."

"That's good." His eyes flicked open. "I don't want to die here, like that." He blinked a couple of times. "Unless you're really an angel."

I frowned. "That's a religious human thing, isn't it?"

"I'm sorry, I didn't meant to offend you," He said

hastily, "I just meant—"

I waved my hand at him in dismissal. "I'm not offended. Human religion is interesting, although some of it is a little weird. Do people really believe in a flying spaghetti monster? Nevermind, that isn't important right now."

He exhaled through his nose. "I suppose it isn't. He rubbed his head and sat up slowly. "I know you said we should wait until morning, but if those things come back…"

I interrupted. "Flying with a sore head might be the last thing you do."

"Staying here might be the last thing we *both* do."

I rubbed my forehead with my fingertips. "I can hold the beetles off while you sleep, if they do come back."

"Summer." He said my name softly, tenderly. "I feel like I've spent too long doing nothing but sleep. I'm ready to live again. Even if I die in the process."

"That's very noble, but it's not very logical."

"Are Fae known for being logical?" he asked.

"Not especially." I smiled. "We're pretty emotional at times and, for those who live for a long time, some of us are dumbasses." I hadn't thought about my sisters for a while. Now I was, I pushed the thought of them away. They were the last ones I wanted on my mind right now.

"Fine, let's go on then." I got to my feet and offered my hand.

"Do you really think those beetles eat bones?" he asked.

I froze. "I don't think so."

"What else might, then?"

I shook my head. "I have no idea. Honestly, I don't think I want to know." My curiosity was mostly insatiable, but not as great as my attachment to my bones.

"Probably something we could step on if we were bigger," he mused.

"Possibly." It might be that easy, and it might not. The sooner we left, the sooner we wouldn't have to worry about it.

"You're not filling me with confidence," he said dryly.

"I'm sorry." I picked up my bag and swung it onto my back. "The Fae realm isn't all rainbows and flowers."

"I don't think I've seen a rainbow since I got here." He put his trembling arms around me. "Plenty of flowers though."

"We do like our flowers," I agreed. "And all the

other plants." We walked to the entrance to the nook and I opened my wings. "Hold on tight."

This time I didn't mind that he squeezed me so hard I could barely breathe. The beetles gave us both a sense of urgency. I couldn't fix lesser magic if I was here, especially if I was a snack for a bunch of bugs.

I soared upward, slowly and carefully. Once in a while I caught sight of a flash of light, twilight, the first stars, then the moon. The last was almost full, casting enough illumination to avoid the worst of the snags.

Once or twice I bumped us into the side of the crack. I winced as a jag of stone scraped my wing. Another time it was Fletcher's arm which was scraped. To his credit, he didn't make a sound beyond a gasp.

"Are you all right?" I asked. His head wound might have left him dazed, or more injured than I realised.

"I'm fine," he ground out. "Are we nearly there?"

I glanced up. "I think so." I *hoped* so. I was getting more and more tired. The strain of carrying him, and my own weight, was telling in every wing beat.

Just as I said that, we burst up out into fresh air and a star-filled sky. I flew us away from the crack and lowered us to the ground.

Around us, blades of grass looked enormous. It grew from the cracks between tiles, like the place we just escaped from.

I let Fletcher go and tried to keep from falling over from the exertion. He grabbed my arm and kept me upright, then helped me to sit.

"I'll make us back to normal size in a moment." I blinked to clear my spinning head. "I just need to rest for a bit."

He sat beside me. The hood was still over his head, but his eyes shone in the moonlight. "I ate all of your food, didn't I? Right when you needed it."

"You needed it more," I said. "I'll be fine. There will be fruit around somewhere." I gestured around weakly. "It'll be easier to find when we're bigger."

I closed my eyes and focused on my breathing. I hadn't done anything so strenuous in…ever.

I felt Fletcher's hand on my shoulder.

"Maybe we should find somewhere to get some rest. You sleep and I'll keep watch. I can stay tiny until you've had some sleep."

I tried to stifle a yawn. "That might be a good idea. I'd hate to accidentally explode us both."

He laughed softly. "I'd hate to be exploded."

"Me too." I looked around, but still had no idea where we were. For all I knew, we were close to the capital. Everything looked different at this size. And this exhaustion.

Where were Huon, Saff and Kale? They could be nearby, or on the other side of the realm. I was certain they hadn't followed me through the trap-door. If they had, I would have seen them. Or heard them at least. Huon and Saff would have made more noise than the beetles.

They might still be there, waiting for me to come back through. On one hand, that would make them easier to find. On the other, they should be finding out the cause of the loss of lesser magic.

I was only one Fae; they had bigger problems than what happened to me.

I sighed. Knowing them, they would have chosen to wait.

"We should find somewhere safer to hide," I said. "Maybe in a space between the tiles." Of course there was no guarantee it would be safer there, but it was less open than here.

"Do you need some help?" He offered his hand and pulled me to my feet. We took a few steps to the edge and looked down. The moonlight showed dirt and grass, but nothing more sinister than that.

I sat on the edge of the tile andslid down into the gap. The ground was soft under my feet.

"This will do."

Fletcher jumped down beside me, pulled off my bag and made me a little place to sleep.

While he sat with his back to the side of the tile, I curled up and nestled down.

"Thank you," I said softly.

"No, thank *you*," he replied. "You saved my ass. A couple of times."

"Yes, well, you would have escaped from there somehow." I suspected the way we had come was the only way.

"Maybe." He shrugged. "Maybe not. Get some sleep."

I closed my eyes. I wasn't sure I could sleep, but an hour or two of rest would help to regain my strength.

I had a feeling I would need it. I had some idea where we might be and it was going to suck for us both if I was right.

CHAPTER TWELVE

*T*he sun hadn't quite peeked over the side of the tile when I awoke. I must have slept for longer than I planned.

I yawned and stretched. My foot bumped into something before I remembered Fletcher.

"Sorry." I opened my eyes and sat up.

He leaned against the tile, his hood drawn tightly around his face with his hands. A pair of eyes peered at me. The rest of him was obscured.

"Are you all right?" I started to move closer, but stopped. I might be what had him on edge.

"No. Yes." His voice was rough.

"Which is it?" I asked lightly. I cocked my head and hoped not to look threatening. Unless he was a beetle, or something else nasty, I was harmless.

Mostly.

He loosened one finger from his hood just enough to point toward the east.

I glanced around, but saw nothing but the sun. Then it dawned on me.

"The light is too bright?"

He nodded. "I'm trying to get used to it slowly, but it's rising fast. Is there something you can do? Some magic or something?"

"I could poke your eyes out." I held out two fingers like prongs. "But that's a bit extreme."

"Just a bit," he agreed. "But there's more." He exhaled through pursed lips. "You haven't seen what I really look like."

I arched an eyebrow at him. "That's true. You're not part beetle are you?"

He snorted a laugh. "Not that I know of."

I raised the other eyebrow. "Now I'm worried," I joked.

After a moment I scooted over closer to him. He drew back slightly, but at least he didn't turn away.

"This might sound strange," I said, as if he hadn't been through enough weird things lately. We were currently the size of his pinkie toe, if he was normal size in the human realm. "I like you. I don't care what you look like."

I put my hands over his and gently drew them away from his face.

They trembled. I held them like that for a few moments, then let go and pushed his hood back a bit.

He flinched and blinked against the sudden glare and the way the left side of his face was revealed to me.

From temple to chin to the top of his beard, his skin was scarred and puckered. The burn must have happened a long time ago, the red had faded to the same peachy shade as the rest of him.

I traced a line down the side of his face with the tip of my finger, across his beard and down his neck.

"What happened?" I asked softly.

"I got pushed into a fire as a kid," he explained.

"Pushed?" I echoed. "That's horrible."

He looked away. "I told you."

"Hey." I moved over, back into his line of sight. "I meant someone doing that to you, not the scars. If you had them all over your face, it wouldn't bother me. Gods know I'm not perfect either."

I lowered my voice to a conspiratorial whisper. "I have one wing bigger than the other."

His mouth quirked. "Really?"

"Really." I nodded. "I can show you if you like." I

spread them out behind me, as best I could in the small space and while seated.

"See?"

He looked at one, then the other. "I see what you mean. The left is slightly smaller."

I sighed dramatically. "Right? It's a wonder I don't fly lopsided."

"They're still beautiful. Can I..."

"Touch them? Sure, just be careful."

"Do they bite?" He eyed them dubiously.

I giggled. "No, they're just... I don't know what word humans use for it. If I'm touched a certain way, it turns me on."

His mouth formed an O. "Erogenous zone?"

"Gods bless you," I replied.

He blinked, then broke into a grin. "I wasn't sneezing, that's just what it's called. Maybe I should —um—wait until I know you a little better first."

I shrugged and lowered my wings. "Suit yourself. We should probably get back to normal size and get out of here. We need to find food, and the others."

"Others?" He rose and helped me to my feet.

I told him about Huon, Saff and Kale.

"So, your lover is the Fae king. And your other lover is his friend. And you like Kale too." He climbed up to the top of the tile and stood beside me.

"Yes, and I like you too. That probably sounds odd to a human." I took his hand.

"No, I've seen *The Bachelorette*."

"The what?"

"Nothing." He waved his spare hand. "So none of them mind?"

"Saff and Huon don't." I grimaced at how annoyed I had been only the day before. Now it seemed petty. But then, I hadn't been attacked by beetles before that. "I haven't really spoken to Kale, but I think he likes me too."

"So, if you and I ever... They wouldn't have a problem with that?"

"I wouldn't think so." I started to grow us back to larger size. "Would you? I mean, my wings don't freak you out? Or my magic?"

He paused. "I find it fascinating. And your wings are gorgeous. *You're* gorgeous."

I blushed. "You're pretty cute yourself."

"Thank you. And thanks for not finding my scars repulsive. Most people stare."

"I'm not most people," I replied. "Technically I'm not people at all."

"I guess Fae are better people than people," he said.

"No, some of us are assholes." I looked down at the tile. It was now the size of a table which might fit ten to twelve diners around it. Whatever had put it there was around the size of a normal human. Or liked really wide tiles.

"Have you got any idea where we are yet?" he asked.

The trees around us wore brown leaves and sagging branches. The smell of off meat was faint, but strong enough to make me wrinkle my nose. The stone tiles at our feet stretched several meters and ended at a crumbling wall. Shattered columns poked up here and there, most covered in moss, or hidden behind grass and weeds.

"Kale said something about an ancient pre-Fae civilisation," I said slowly. "This could be the remains of that. If so, we're more likely to meet—"

An arrow whizzed over my head. It missed me by a finger's width.

"Trolls."

I grabbed his arm and fell into a crouch. "We need to get to cover."

"Can't you just blast them apart with your magic?"

"No, trolls are harder to kill." Another arrow flew over my head. "Evidently their aim sucks." That was fortunate. I didn't much feel like being skewered. Not with an arrow anyway.

"But they are trying to kill us?" he asked.

"Oh, very much so," I replied. "Trolls eat anything."

"Geez, and they say everything in Australia is trying to kill me," he muttered. "All right, how about the trees straight in front?"

I glanced up. The leaves were so rotten they looked ready to drop from the branches. The trunks were thick enough to provide cover.

"They'll do, but don't touch the foliage." If it burnt my skin, there was no telling what it would do to his. "On three. One. Two."

An arrow grazed my arm.

"Three!"

We rose and sprinted for the trees. Once we stepped off the stones, the ground was soft and spongy. With every step, I felt like I might sink into the dirt and become stuck. I could fly myself out, but carrying Fletcher would make it harder.

We reached the trees and almost fell over each other behind the trunks.

"You're hurt." He panted.

"It's nothing." The arrowhead had taken off the top layer of skin. A bead of blood rose in the graze and threatened to trickle over.

"They don't use poison on those things, do they?" Fletcher peered around the trunk.

"Not that I know of." I was more worried about the leaves which hung just above my head. "How many are there?"

"Three," he replied. "No, four. I'm no psychologist, but these guys look angry. And hungry. Maybe hangry."

I snorted. "According to Kale, we're related to them. You'd think they'd be nicer to their own kind."

"Hmmm." Fletcher looked back at me. "I see a resemblance. Sort of. They are getting closer though. Do we fight these guys or keep running?"

I hesitated. I had only seen trolls from a distance before, and in books. "I don't think we can take on four of them. We're smarter, but they're bigger. What do you do?"

He frowned at me. "What do you mean?"

"You have trolls in the human realm, don't you? How do you deal with them?"

"Oh. In a way we do. We block them, but I don't think that will work here."

"Block them?" I frowned at him.

"It's—I'll explain later. Can you make us big so we can step on them?"

I grimaced. "I'd prefer not to have to wipe troll from the bottom of my boots, but that gives me an idea."

"Why does that make me a little nervous?" he asked.

I grinned. "Because you've known me for just enough to know I'm a kickass Fae."

He grinned back and my heart flipped. He was hotter than all the hells, especially with his scars.

"That's true," he said. "Now what do you have in mind?"

I grabbed his hand, pulled him over to me and whispered in his ear.

He nodded. "All right, sounds like a plan."

The trolls got closer. They stomped through the dirt with heavy steps and grunts that passed for communication. They could speak Fae, according to the books, if they bothered, but preferred to rely on simple sounds and hand signals instead.

In some ways, I related to this. I certainly preferred to rely on grunts until I had my first cup of tea for the day. It was safer that way, for everyone.

The lead troll appeared around the trunk. He—I presumed by the lack of breasts on his bare chest—stopped and looked around. His leathery face scrunched up in a scowl.

He turned around and growled, deep in his throat.

Another troll, this one with breasts hanging heavy, growled in return. She sniffed the air and turned in a slow circle. She made a cutting gesture with her hand and waved at the male.

He shrank back from her and whimpered like a scared animal.

She hissed at him and he scurried away with surprising agility.

The female troll grunted to herself and stomped off after him.

"I almost feel sorry for him," Fletcher whispered into my ear.

I hardly dared to move, in case they saw us, but I snorted softly. "Don't. He would eat you for his next meal. He might not even make sure you're dead first."

The female troll stopped and turned back, her breasts swinging. Her eyes narrowed. She scanned the ground and moved to peer behind a tree.

I held my breath as she passed right under us. Partly because I didn't want her to hear me and partly because she smelled like dirty feet.

She shook her head. Her pale, greasy hair flicked back and forth. It looked as wet as the leaves around us. Was that a coincidence, or was the loss of lesser magic affecting them in some way we hadn't realised yet?

Maybe she didn't believe in personal hygiene.

She let out a gusty sigh and trudged off after the other trolls.

I sagged in relief. The branch we sat on swayed with the movement and Fletcher grabbed my arm to keep from falling off.

"That was close," he whispered. "If she'd looked up—"

"Thank the gods she didn't," I agreed.

"Thank *you*," he said. "If you hadn't made us small enough to hide in the branches, we might be being eaten by now. And not in a good way."

I smiled. "I give that innuendo a seven."

"I'll keep working on those," he said. Meanwhile, he leaned over to press his lips gently to mine.

"You do that." I kissed him back. My tongue tasted his lips and flicked against his teeth.

"I will," he said against my mouth. He drew away reluctantly. "But first, we should find some food."

"Agreed, I'm starving." And I needed to find the others. The graze where the arrow hit me started to sting.

CHAPTER THIRTEEN

"I don't understand. Surely if we're small and eat something like a berry, we'll stay full." Fletcher squinted at me.

Given the state of the trees, it had taken us the better part of two hours to find a plant healthy enough to trust its fruit. The patch of blackberries, which looked ready to strangle the other plants around them, was a welcome find.

"It doesn't work that way," I explained. I was calm, in spite of the increasing pain in my arm. It seemed to be spreading. Slowly, but still...

"If you grow, the berry remains the same size. Worse luck, since this would keep us for a month." Assuming I lived that long.

"In fact I'll put us back as we were. I think it's as

safe as it's going to get and picking berries will be easier if we're not the same size as them."

"Do you ever get confused?" He took my hand.

"Frequently," I replied. "But I suspect you were asking about something in particular."

He chuckled. "Sorry. Yes, I meant, how do you know what size you're supposed to be?"

"Ah." I started to make us the size we were when we met. "I just stick to being the same size I usually am. Most Fae do the same, unless we visit the human realm. When we could do that."

"Right, but things here seem to be the same size as they are there. The plants and flowers. Even the ruins. But the Fae stay smaller."

"Fae are environmentally friendly." I released his hand and started picking berries. One fit in my hand and smelled divine.

I took a tiny bite and chewed. My mouth didn't burn, so I took a bigger bite. Juice trickled down my chin.

"Let me get that for you," Fletcher offered.

I thought he was going to wipe my face with his sleeve, but he leaned his face closer to me and licked my chin.

"There, that's got it." He grinned.

I waited.

He frowned for a moment, then smiled. "This is where I say I liked the taste of your juice, isn't it?"

I shrugged and gave him a smile. "It could have, but I think the moment passed."

"No score for Fletcher then." He pouted playfully.

"Not this time." I patted his arm. "I'm sure another opportunity will arise."

"Seven," he said.

I blinked. "Did you just rate *my* innuendo?"

"It seems fair, if you're rating mine." He bit into his own berry.

"That was so much better than a seven." I planted a hand on my hip.

He eyed me. "Fine. Seven point two?"

I cocked my head. "Point two?"

"You don't have decimals here?"

I looked at him in confusion and shook my head slowly. I wasn't sure if he was serious or not. Humans were odd at times. This was one of those times.

"Um. They're parts of whole numbers," he explained. "Like if this berry was a number and then it got cut up into ten pieces. Two of those pieces would be point two. At least, that's how I understand it. I'm no mathematician."

I thought about it for a few moments. "So you're saying it was only slightly better than a seven?"

"Exactly." He toasted me with his half-eaten berry.

"Maybe that's what happened to lesser magic," I mused. "It closed the veil to save us from ridiculous ideas like numbers having points."

He burst out laughing. "In that case, I'm on the right side. I should have come here in high school. Being in the dark might have been better than learning calculus or algebra."

"I don't know what those are, but they can't be worse than being stuck down there," I said.

He sighed. "I guess not. There are certainly better places to be stuck. Like here with you, eating giant berries." He leaned in to kiss my cheek.

"I've never met anyone like you," he said softly.

"Is that a good thing or a bad thing?" I asked, only half teasing.

"It's a fantastic thing." He cupped my cheek and gently ran a thumb up and down my skin. "Smart, beautiful and kickass. What a combination. And you're not repulsed by me. At least, I don't think you are."

I smiled and leaned into his hand. "I think you're sweet."

His face fell slightly.

"And sexy."

He brightened.

I stood on my toes and lightly kissed his mouth.

He ran a hand up my arm. When he touched my graze, I hissed in pain and drew back.

"I'm sorry, I didn't mean—" His eyes widened. He grabbed my hand and pulled it toward him.

The graze was now inflamed; red skin surrounded it for several centimetres. The whole area felt hot and stung badly.

"This doesn't look good," he said. "Why didn't you say something?"

I didn't appreciate his accusing tone. "Are you a healer?" I replied defensively.

"No, but… We should have found you help before we found food. Or wasted time talking about pointless things like decimals."

"I thought that was the one *with* points," I joked weakly.

He frowned. "What can I do for you? If you need to leave me here and fly off—"

I interrupted. "I'm not leaving you here alone."

"Well, what then? How do we find a healer?" he asked.

"I'm not sure where we are," I admitted. "If we could find the others..."

"Then that's what we'll do." He nodded. "Do you have the energy to make me a bit bigger?"

"What for?" I asked.

"So I can carry you." He held up a finger. "You've saved my ass twice. It's time to return the favour. Besides, the less you do, the less that will spread."

I wanted to argue, but he was right. About that last bit at least.

"Fine. But only a little bit bigger. It will use up energy to do too much." Frankly, I was tired already. Whatever was in that arrow had slowly entered my system and started to travel around my body. I needed to rest and get help. There was no way I was going to let myself die until we restored lesser magic.

I put a hand on his arm and enlarged him by half again.

"There's something I need to do first." He slipped off his hoodie and then the shirt he wore underneath.

My eyes widened. He must have been working out down there in the dark. Every centimetre of him was toned and firm. His left shoulder and down his arm was covered in scars like his face, but his other arm was covered in tattoos. For some reason, that surprised me.

"Is that a fairy?" I pointed to one.

He looked down at the picture of a winged woman hovering on his bicep. "What can I say, I always had a thing for Tinker Bell."

"Who?" And why did I feel a stab of jealousy? That wasn't like me at all.

"She was a character from *Peter Pan*," he replied. "It's a book," he added when I gave him a blank look.

"Oh. I love books." Maybe I should have stayed in the capital instead of coming on this crazy adventure which might kill me.

"Me too, that's why I work in a library." He put his hoodie back on and started picking blackberries. He bundled them up in his shirt and handed it to me. "That's for later."

"Good thinking." I nodded. I might not keep down the ones I'd eaten, much less eat more, but he would need some nourishment.

"It happens from time to time." He gave me a smile, then crouched. "Can you climb onto my back?"

I gave him a funny look.

He blushed and rose. "Sorry, I forgot you have wings."

I probably should have taken him up on his offer, but with some effort I fluttered up high enough to wind my legs around his waist and wrap my hands around his neck. I leaned my chest against his back and placed my head on his shoulder.

He put his hands under my ass to help support me.

"Comfortable?" he asked.

"I'd prefer a sedan chair, but it'll do," I said, careful not to speak too loudly in his ear.

He chuckled. "I didn't know you had those in the Fae realm."

I wanted to point out that if we didn't get lesser magic back, he would have to start thinking of the realm as his home too, but I didn't. He might get pissed off at the thought, and that wouldn't help either of us.

"We have books from the human realm," I replied. "I've read about them."

"Oh. What else have you read about?" He started to walk in a roughly easterly direction.

"Dragons," I replied. "Women with hair so long a prince can climb up it. Women with fish tails instead of legs."

"Mermaids," he said. "So, fairy tales?"

"I guess so," I agreed. "I once read a book about

people who flew amongst the stars and met creatures from other worlds."

"Ah, science fiction. I don't mind a bit of that. And fantasy. I didn't expect to be living it someday though."

He stepped around some rocks and down a slope.

I began to shiver. I gritted my teeth and tried to contain it. I didn't want him to worry about me. Well, no more than he already was.

"Are you all right?" He must have felt me tremble.

"As well as I can be, under the circumstances. Maybe we should keep talking." In spite of that, I closed my eyes and nestled in closer.

"I think this is where I say you need to stay with me." He stopped walking. "Summer?"

I murmured. "I'm still here. I don't die that easily. Just keep talking."

"All right." He quickened the pace and chatted about everything from the weather to the books he preferred.

I only half-listened, but mostly focused on his voice and how pleasant it was. His accent was different to any humans I had met before, but it was sexy as hells. Or would be if I didn't feel like shit.

"Crap," he swore suddenly.

"What?" My eyes popped open.

"Trolls."

"I can try to shrink us down…"

"It's too late, they've seen us."

Six trolls stepped out of the trees and surrounded us, knives and knocked arrows all pointed at us.

"Well, fuck, this sucks."

CHAPTER FOURTEEN

Fletcher lowered me to the ground and shielded me with his body. My knees almost buckled underneath me, but I caught myself at the last moment.

"We don't want any trouble." He raised his hands to either side. "We're just passing through on the way to—"

"You're not Fae."

Cautiously, I looked around him.

A troll woman had stepped forward and now eyed him warily. Her gaze snapped toward me and she pointed a thick, stubby finger at me.

"Why did you do this?" she demanded.

"You're going to have to elaborate." I moved out from behind Fletcher and crossed my arms. I winced and lowered them again. My graze felt worse. A sheen of sweat covered me from head to toe. In spite of that, I was freezing cold. Feverish, no doubt.

"I'm not at my best today." I wobbled slightly.

Fletcher put out a hand to steady me.

"The Fae took away lesser magic," the troll declared. "The plants are dying. Because of *you*."

I blinked. "No, we didn't." I hadn't expected her to say anything like that, but now I thought about it, it made sense. We suspected them after all. Maybe we should have sent someone to speak to them. Although, they did tend to attack first and ask questions later.

"We're out here trying to figure out what happened, so we can fix it," I explained.

She frowned at me, clearly doubtful, then asked, "Why should we believe you?"

"Why else would we be out here?" I countered.

"Can you help her?" Fletcher blurted. "A troll arrow hit her. It seems to have had some kind of poison on it." He gestured for me to show her.

"I think you've read too many books," I muttered from the side of my mouth. Did he really think they'd help me?

Reluctantly, I held up my arm. The inflammation spread almost to my elbow.

Maybe if I cut that part of my arm off—

"We can fix her," the troll woman said with a curt nod. "But I see no reason to." She lifted her chin.

"How about compassion?" Fletcher asked.

"These are trolls," I reminded him. "They don't care about Fae. I'm surprised they even travel together."

"Fae understand nothing," the woman growled. "You think you're better than us. You think of us like we're animals."

I couldn't disagree, so I shrugged.

"Prove her wrong," Fletcher said insistently. "Heal her, then we can all work together to fix lesser magic."

The troll woman and I both shot him a look, then exchanged them with each other.

"You think trolls and Fae can work together?" The woman looked incredulous. "Fae are too selfish."

"I can work with anyone, if it means we find the answer to this." I locked gazes with her and stared until she looked away. "We both need lesser magic back before the whole realm dies."

She didn't answer.

I sighed and started to turn away. "I guess trolls can't put their pride aside, even if it means we all die."

"Wait!" she called out after us. "I would rather work with a Fae than see our children die out. I will heal you."

I turned back. "Really?"

She scowled, but nodded and gestured toward a troll man who stood behind her.

"I am Korta. This is Lun. He makes the poison. He knows the cure."

Lun didn't look too happy, but he pulled a pouch off his belt, opened it and offered me a small jar with a leather stopper. He held up two fingers and waved at the jar before he handed it to me.

"Two drops?" I asked.

He frowned and shook his head, then looked to Korta as though asking her to save him from stupid Fae.

Yeah, fuck you too, buddy.

She shook her head and nodded at him to keep trying.

He sighed heavily, then mimed drinking.

"Two gulps?" I asked. "Are you sure it's safe?"

Lun growled and made to lunge at me.

Korta snapped something and he held himself back, but gave me a filthy look.

"Lun takes pride in his work and his honour.

Poisoning an ally, even a Fae, would dishonour him and his family for seven generations."

"That's specific," Fletcher said.

"It is the way of the troll," Korta declared. "Drink."

What was the worst that could happen? If I didn't take the potion, I might die anyway. I removed the stopper and took a sniff. It smelled tangy, like oranges, with a sweet undertone.

"It smells nice," I said to Fletcher.

"It's medicine, it will probably taste terrible," he replied.

"Thanks for the words of encouragement."

While he looked apologetic, I took a gulp, then another. It actually tasted pleasant, but burned all the way down my throat. It hit my stomach and threatened to come straight back up.

I coughed and swallowed, but managed to keep everything down.

Lun sidled forward and took back the jar, then motioned for me to sit down. He raised a hand and held it sideways across the sky just under the sun.

I frowned for a moment, then said, "Oh, that's how long it'll take to work?"

He nodded vigorously, pale hair falling over his eyes. He pushed it back and again motioned for me to sit.

"I might as well, I guess." I lowered myself to the ground. He crouched beside me and tucked the jar away.

"You don't talk?" I asked for something to say.

He shook his head and mimed something I didn't understand.

"He swore a vow of silence after his wife died," Korta said. She and the rest of the trolls sat down around us.

Lun nodded sadly. His eyes actually glistened.

"Oh, I'm sorry to hear that," I said, genuinely sad for him. "I'm sure she was… lovely."

Lun nodded. He held out his hands in front of his chest and cupped the air.

"Men never change," Fletcher remarked.

"Human and Fae men value large breasts?" Korta asked.

"Many human men do," Fletcher agreed.

"Fae men as well," I said. "I guess we're not as different as we thought."

Korta looked as though the idea left a bad taste in her mouth. "Perhaps."

"Do the others talk?" The other four, two women and two men, sat and watched, but their hands were on their weapons. At a word from Korta, Fletcher and I would be dead. If they wanted to kill us, they could have, I reasoned, but it wasn't too late for us to accidentally say something offensive.

"They speak when they're permitted to speak," Korta replied curtly.

"You're their leader?" Fletcher asked.

She drew herself up. "I am. I lead a band of a hundred."

"That's impressive." I wiped my brow with my sleeve, but most of the sweat had dried. My trembling stopped and I wasn't quite so cold. Whatever the antidote was, it seemed to be working. "Where are the rest of them?"

Korta smiled savagely. "Hunting another group of Fae."

I blanched. "They don't happen to have mimicat with them, did they?"

Her eyes narrowed. "They did. They are allies of yours?"

"Yes," I said quickly. My heart pounded, which left me feeling sick and dizzy. "Which would make them yours as well."

She fixed me with a long and slightly sour look. For a moment I thought she might deny or dismiss me. She exhaled through pursed lips, gave a nod and gestured toward two of her companions. She snapped something at them and they hurried off through the trees.

"Your friends?" Fletcher whispered.

"Unless there's another group of Fae traveling with a mimicat," I replied.

He quirked an eyebrow at me. "Is that uncommon?"

"Very," I replied. "Mimicats are strange and not to be trusted."

"Not unlike Fae," Korta said, dryly.

I forced a laugh. "Right, just like us Fae."

"My words weren't meant to be humorous." She looked at me through half-lidded eyes, no hint of amusement.

"Oh, I know," I said sweetly. "But we all need each other, like it or not. We have to work together for the good of the whole realm. That also means being civil to one another. Wouldn't you agree?" The steady look I gave her covered how weak I felt, although the potion was working bit by bit.

"I have saved your life and may spare your allies," Korta replied, her tone stony to match her expression. "That is civility to trolls. We see nothing rude in speaking the truth."

"What do you consider rude then?" Fletcher asked. He glanced at me and shrugged. "Just curious."

"Those who question our honour," Korta replied. "Honour is everything to us. And honesty. Lies are nothing but illusions, tricks."

"So, you don't care for mimicats either," I said flatly.

"They are vermin," she replied, "but tasty." She grinned savagely.

I grimaced. "I'll have to take your word for it. Khat is obnoxious, but we need his help as well. So if you don't eat him, that would be great."

Fletcher raised a finger.

"That wasn't an innuendo," I told him.

He lowered his hand. "I knew that. I just thought maybe you needed cheering up. How are you feeling?" He rubbed my back lightly.

"A little bit better," I replied. "I'll be much better when I know the others are all right."

Korta had pulled out a knife and was cleaning under her nails. "They will be unharmed. If my scouts reach them in time. If not—" She didn't seem too upset by the alternative.

"This might be the shortest alliance in the history of the realm," I muttered.

"Perhaps so," she agreed, "but we will not be the ones to break it."

"Because of your honour?" Fletcher asked.

"Exactly. Evidently humans are more wise than Fae. Are you linked?" Korta looked at him through her eyelashes.

"Linked?" he echoed.

"Yes. Uh—" She seemed to search for the right word.

"Married," I supplied. "I think she's flirting with you." To be honest I wanted the answer to that question too. Although we only knew each other a matter of hours, I felt attached to him, like the gods had destined us to meet.

"Oh." He blinked rapidly. His eyes must have adjusted to the light, he looked less uncomfortable, but he was clearly rattled by the question. "No, not married. But I…um…" He blushed.

"I think he just wants to be friends with you," I told Korta.

She curled her lip at me, but flashed Fletcher a smile. "Very well, human. It's your loss. Korta is a wonderful lover."

"I'm sure," he murmured. "But my name is Fletcher."

Now she seemed surprised. "You make arrows?"

He chuckled. "No, it's just my name. Us human sometimes name babies after occupations. Like Cooper or Hunter."

"Hunter." Korta nodded her approval. "Is it their wish for their child to become a warrior?"

"Maybe," he agreed. "Or maybe they just like the name."

She sniffed. "Hmmm, I think maybe humans are peculiar after all."

"We can be," he agreed. "Some boys are named Dick. That would be a lot to live up to."

I snorted. "Do humans also name their children breast?"

He grinned "Not that I know of. Dick is short for Richard. Like Sum is short for Summer."

I frowned. "How do you get Dick from Richard?"

"You be nice to him, I suppose." Fletcher wiggled his eyebrows at me.

For a moment I stared at him, then I laughed. "That is a terrible joke. You get no points for that."

Korta looked at us both like we were crazy. "You talk too much." She waved her fingers at me. "You should be resting. If you don't heal, Lun's honour will be in question."

Lun nodded and gave me a dark look as though I would be completely to blame if I died.

"Well, we wouldn't want that." I leaned against Fletcher, who put an arm around me and held me close. His touch was warm and gentle, familiar like we'd known each other for years. In some way, it reminded me of Huon. Comfortable, but without the bickering which kept our relationship exciting.

"Oh, here you are." Khat's drawl interrupted my thoughts. "I should have known you'd already be prisoners. Did they sneak up while you were screwing?"

I blushed and sat up straight again. The trolls herded Huon, Saff and Kale through the trees. Khat walked beside Huon.

Huon's expression went from furious to relieved when he saw me. Saff grinned. Only Kale seemed unperturbed.

"We were eating," I told Khat. Not that I owed him an explanation of any kind.

I rose with Fletcher's help and moved to embrace all three of the Fae men, Huon last of all. One of his arms lingered around me while he looked me in the face.

"Are you all right?"

"Why, were you worried?" I arched my eyebrows at him.

"Of course not." He rolled his eyes. "Although now I think about it, the trolls *could* have killed you once they learned how annoying you are."

I swatted him on the shoulder. "If that's the case,

then your life expectancy will be much shorter than mine."

"Sounds about right," Saff said. "I've personally threatened him three times in the last hour."

"Four," Kale remarked.

Saff pointed toward him. "You're right. I said if this was a trap he'd led us into, I would stab him in the balls and let him bleed out."

"So," I said to Fletcher, "these are the guys I told you about."

Saff glanced around me. "Oh, hello, Fletch."

"You two know each other?" I asked.

"I think we should sit down," Huon suggested. "We clearly have a lot to talk about."

CHAPTER FIFTEEN

"*H*ow is your arm feeling?" Kale asked softly.

I turned from the fire the trolls built to look at him. Flames flickered and danced in his eyes, but I saw his concern as well.

"Much better," I replied. "It's just a graze again now." I held it up for him to look.

He inspected it, then nodded. "You got lucky. If the arrow hit close to your heart, you wouldn't be here now."

I shuddered. "You're lucky too. If Korta hadn't sent her scouts to find you…"

Saff and Huon already told the tale of how they'd been surrounded by trolls and Khat claimed to have caught them for the trolls. Of course, the trolls hadn't bought a word the mimicat said.

"We would have fought our way out," Kale assured me. He lowered his voice and added, "I was determined to find you." His breath brushed over my cheek, warm and musky.

My heart skipped a beat, then raced frantically. "You were? I'm glad you did. I was worried you'd follow me through the portal."

He looked rueful. "I was tempted, but after I talked Saff and Huon out of touching the trapdoor, I couldn't do it myself. We had no way of knowing where you'd ended up, or if you were alive. I was willing to take the risk," he added in a whisper.

"Lesser magic comes first," I said firmly. I was pleased at his admission though, especially the part where he stopped the others from doing something stupid.

"In my head, I know that," he said. "But my heart..." He swallowed audibly. "Maybe I shouldn't say this. I know you and the others—"

"They know I care about all of you," I assured him. "I understand if you don't want to get involved with someone who is kind of involved with two... or three other men. I mean, it is a little messy." Was 'involved' the right word? Huon was the only one I'd known longer than a couple of days. No one ever said I didn't jump in with both feet.

Kale put a hand on my shoulder and leaned in to kiss me on the mouth. His lips were soft and warm, surprisingly gentle for such a burly Fae.

I kissed him back, lightly at first, then with more heat. His tongue teased my lips apart.

"Not you too," Khat complained. He shoved himself between us and flopped down before he started to groom himself.

"Do you mind?" I asked him.

"No, not at all," the mimicat replied, unperturbed.

I shot Kale an apologetic look.

He shrugged and grimaced at the mimicat, but before he could reply, Huon spoke.

"So, Saff, are you going to tell us how you and Fletcher know each other?"

Part of me wanted to sneak away from the fire with Kale, but I wanted to hear this too.

Fletcher looked uncomfortable with so many others around him, but at least the trolls sat at their own fire, a few metres away. Hospitality apparently only went so far.

"My sister, Tigerlily, stole him and brought him here," Saff said.

"That makes sense." Huon nodded. "He wouldn't have followed *you* here." He grinned.

Saff picked up the closest thing to hand—one of his shoes— and threw it at Huon. The shoe struck him on the shoulder and bounced. It landed a centimetre from the fire.

"That would have served you right," Khat remarked.

"He's right, you know," I said.

"I regret nothing." Saff grabbed up his shoe and placed it beside the other, a safe distance from the flames. "Except that I didn't follow you. It might have been fun. Three of us in the dark like that."

"It wasn't fun," I said firmly.

"Anything but," Fletcher agreed. "And Tigerlily didn't steal me, I came willingly." He glanced at me, an eyebrow raised.

"Eight," I told him.

He pumped the air with his fist.

Saff and Huon exchanged glances and shrugged.

"Then, in typical Tigerlily fashion, she got bored," Saff guessed. "No offence, " he added quickly.

"None taken," Fletcher replied. "I was just as bad, looking for adventure in a strange land."

"You found it," I said as gently as I could.

"And then some," he agreed. "But I prefer this to

being down in the—whatever that place was. Do any of you know?"

"Without getting a closer look—" Kale started.

"No," I interrupted. "You don't want to go down there." After a beat, I added, "Into the cave," in case they thought that was another innuendo.

"Why not?" Huon asked. "You found the way out easily enough."

"All we need is more light and we could have a good look around," Saff added.

Huon nodded his agreement.

"At the risk of agreeing with those two jesters," Khat said, "they might be right."

"There's nothing to see," I argued. "Just a keyhole and no key."

"Did you say we need a key?" A troll moved closer to the fire and crouched just inside its glow. Her intense gaze caught my eyes and held them.

"We?" I asked.

She nodded and held out her hand. "Tavar," she said.

I assumed that was her name. I shook her hand and said, "Summer."

Her brow twitched. "That's not a usual Fae name."

"So everyone keeps reminding me," I said dryly. "I didn't want to be named after flora, all right?"

Tavar seemed amused. "Very well. You are the leader of this band of Fae?"

Saff made a choking noise. "You hear that, Huon?"

"I heard." Huon grinned. "I'm the leader. Summer just likes to think she is."

I rolled my eyes. "Whatever. Let's just get back to the 'we' part."

"And the key," Kale said. "What do you know of it?"

Tavar sat and crossed her legs. "It's a legend amongst the trolls. Since we are allies, I may speak of it to you. Korta has given her permission."

I nodded and gestured for her to go on.

"The ruins due west of here belonged to the Risi. The ancestors of both our people. They were folk of great magic and passion, but also great pride. They fought amongst themselves, especially when their young began to be born without wings. They became known as the trullen. The winged ones, the devallan wanted to drive them out."

Her face showed little expression, but I suspected she was thinking we were still doing the same thing.

"Some claimed a faction of the devallan were doing magic to create the trullen because they wanted slaves. Called the nympha—"

I hissed.

Tavar stopped and regarded me blandly.

"That word is highly offensive to Fae," I said around gritted teeth.

Tavar inclined her head. "Amongst the trolls as well. Although it's often used to describe the Fae."

I bristled.

Kale reached over Khat to put a hand on my arm. "We should listen," he said.

"Oh, I am listening," I replied. This might be a short alliance if the trolls were going to use ugly words against us.

"The nympha," Tavar repeated firmly, "were a race apart from either trullen or devallan. Selfish, ruthless, lazy, they considered themselves above the others. They went too far and were eventually imprisoned and their dark magic was outlawed. Every book, every scroll, every potion was destroyed. Everything which could be, at least."

"What do you mean everything that could be?" Fletcher looked enraptured.

Tavar shrugged. "Some artefacts resisted everything: fire, magic, hammers. Eventually they were locked away. The key was hidden so no one could find it and open it."

"You think those artefacts have something to do with lesser magic?" Kale asked.

The blood drained from my face. "That door. You think they're down there? That would explain why there's only one way out."

"There should be *no* way out," Tavar said. "The dark magic has made a crack."

"And sucked lesser magic down into the vault storing the artefacts," Saff said.

All eyes turned to him.

He shrugged. "It makes sense, doesn't it?"

"Yes, it does," Kale said thoughtfully. "Perhaps if we can get in there, we can release the lesser magic."

Silence fell for a moment as the enormity of his words sank in.

"Why didn't we know any of this?" I asked finally. "Risi, Trullen, Devallen?"

"We did," Huon said softly.

I swung my head to stare at him. "What do you mean?"

"Birch kept a library hidden in his room. Only he and I knew. And Mother. The books in there told the history of the Fae. The real history."

I blinked. "What the fuck, Huon? Why would he keep that from us?"

From me.

"Fae trying enslave Fae. Virtual genocide of our own people. It was a long time ago and it's ugly." He looked down toward the fire.

For the longest time, I had no words. Then I shook my head slowly and said, "The truth isn't always pretty, but we had a right to know."

Huon glanced up. "Birch didn't agree. Nor did his father, or his—"

"And what do *you* think?" I asked.

"I hadn't given it any thought." He sighed. "Summer, it was a thousand years ago. It has nothing to do with now."

"On the contrary," Kale said softly. "It has everything to do with it. Did the books mention artefacts or a key?"

"Keys," Tavar said.

Now I stared at her. "I beg your pardon, did you say *keys?* Plural?"

"Yes, three of them in fact. One in the Fae part of the realm, one in troll territory—"

"If you say the last is in the human realm…" I rubbed my forehead with my fingertips.

"So the legend goes."

"Has anyone got a vat of wine?" I wasn't sure if I wanted to drink it or drown in it. Maybe both. "The last key is in a place we can't get to and the whole realm will die without it?"

Tavar hesitated and looked over her shoulder toward her companions. "There may be a way to get to the human realm."

"How?" Saff asked.

"Same question," Fletcher said. He looked less eager than I might have expected for someone who had just learnt there might be a way home.

"Does it involve a cave full of screamspinners?" Khat asked.

"No, but the troll key is kept in such a cave," Tavar replied.

"Of course it is," I said.

"Korta wants me to show you," Tavar added. "And give you whatever help you need."

"The whole band isn't coming with us?" I asked. No one at the other fire was even looking in our direction.

"Screamspinners are sacred to trolls. Entering their territory is considered sacrilege."

"So they're scared," Khat asked dryly.

"Trolls prefer not to be eaten," Tavar said with a hint of annoyance.

"Funny, mimicats feel the same way," Khat said in Tavar's voice.

Her hand went to the knife at her hip, but she didn't pull it out. Instead she narrowed her eyes at the mimicat.

"If you want to maintain this alliance, you would be better to show some respect to me and the rest of the trolls."

"Right back at you," Khat said, unperturbed. "If you're afraid of screamspinners, it seems you need us as much as we need you. More so, because we could find a cave by ourselves. Am I not right?"

"Both of you, stop," Huon said.

I'd never heard him sound so forceful before. It was kinda hot.

"For the good of all of us, we need to get along. No more antagonising each other. Understood?"

"Can I still tease you?" Saff asked.

Huon knitted his brows. "Yes, but no being a dick."

"It's a fine line." Saff shrugged.

"It is, but I'll tell you if you cross it."

"All right, deal."

I rolled my eyes. "We should get some sleep. I have a feeling tomorrow will be a long day."

If I could sleep, with everything now swirling around in my head.

CHAPTER SIXTEEN

I managed to sleep for a few hours, but woke with the moon still high in the sky. I tossed and turned for a while. Wide awake, but not wanting to disturb the others who slept beside the fire, I rose and snuck off just outside the flame's light.

I lowered myself to sit on a flat rock and tugged my blanket around my shoulders. Even from here, I heard Saff snoring. The sound made me smile. At least he was getting some rest.

"You can't sleep either?"

Huon's voice made me jump so hard I thought my heart would burst out of my chest.

"Gods!" I managed to whisper, in spite of my fright. "What the hells, Huon?"

"Sorry." He flopped down beside me and put an arm around me. "I thought you could use the company. My head is spinning, so I know yours must be in a whirl."

I leaned against him. He smelled of spices and warm earth.

"Why didn't you tell me about Birch's library?" I asked. "Why didn't he?" That cut most of all. I thought he trusted and cared about me. Now I knew he had kept such a big secret from me, I wondered what else he'd held back.

"I didn't know it was important," Huon replied. "And…"

"Yes?" I prompted.

"I was being selfish. I figured I shared you with enough books. If you'd known about those, you would have spent months in there reading them all."

"I probably would," I agreed, "and we might have more answers than we do now."

"We might not," he countered. "Birch had no more answers than we do, or he would have told us."

"That's true," I conceded. "Maybe he was ashamed of the past."

"It seems like we all should be," Huon agreed.

"That begs one question," I mused. "Why not try to make amends with the trolls? He was as hateful about them as any of us. And as wrong." As strange as they were, they were not the animals I assumed.

"I don't know," Huon replied. "Maybe all the hate was to keep the keys apart."

"Maybe. Or maybe we're just assholes."

"That is possible," he agreed. "That would mean trolls are too."

"They seem to be nicer than we are," I said.

"Are you planning to run off with one?" he asked, teasingly.

"I'll think about it." I straightened the blanket around my knees. "Maybe I'll run off with several."

He chuckled, then cupped my chin to turn my face toward him. When he pressed his mouth to mine, my lips were already apart, ready for his probing tongue. I sucked the tip gently and then gave it a playful nip.

He pulled back just far enough to say, "I was scared." He kissed me. "When you disappeared." Kiss. "I didn't think I would see you again." Kiss.

He pried the blanket apart and ran his hands lightly over the fabric of my shirt where it covered my breasts. When my nipples responded to his touch, he massaged them with his thumbs.

"And yet, here I am," I replied, a little breathless.

"With a human in tow." He tugged down the front

of my shirt to expose one nipple, then leaned in to run the tip of his tongue over it.

"Is that a problem?" I arched my back and pushed my breast forward.

"Not for me." He untied the front of my shirt and pushed it aside before slowly massaging my breasts. His palm rubbed against the hard pebbles my nipples became under his touch. "Will I be sharing you with him as well?"

"It's possible. I like him too." I tried to gauge his reaction, but thinking was becoming more difficult.

"As long as you don't forget me." He kissed my cheek, then tickled his way down my cheek with his tongue. He ran it lightly over my neck, then gave me a sharp nip. "Something to remember me by."

"As if I could forget you." I reached down to rub my hand over his hard cock, which strained to be free of his pants. "You're way too much of a brat to forget that easily."

He laughed, his breath hot on my neck. "That's funny, I thought the same about you. Take my cock out."

"I'm sure you did." I unbuttoned his pants and freed his cock. "In your case, it's true though." I wrapped my fingers around his erection.

"You can say anything you like when you have my cock in your hand." He moved against me.

"Oh really?" I pushed his pants down and moved to kneel in the soft earth beside the rock. "What about now?" I licked the tip of his cock, tasting a drop of his warm pre-cum on the tip.

"You can not only say anything, but I'll agree with it." He panted.

I slipped my mouth over his tip and sucked gently.

He ran a hand over my hair, then curled his fingers into it, holding me there lightly.

I sucked him in a little deeper. One hand curled around his base, the other stroked his balls.

He groaned. "Your mouth lives up to your name."

I laughed around his cock and sucked harder.

Slowly, he eased himself out a little, then thrust into my mouth. His cock reached the back of my throat before he pulled out and thrust in again. Over and over he slid in and out with ever increasing urgency.

His face was barely illuminated by moonlight, but enough that I could watch his face as I sucked. His eyes were closed and his mouth drawn back in concentration. His eyelids fluttered as they always did when he was about to come.

"Harder," he moaned.

I massaged his balls harder, my hand moving back and forth as they followed his cock between my lips. I sucked harder, deeper.

"Good girl, I'm going to—" His eyes shot open and fixed on mine as he frantically fucked my mouth. With a grunt, he came. His salty cum squirted into my throat like a wave of warm honey.

"Swallow it," he ground it.

Without breaking eye contact, I swallowed it down, then pulled my face back from him.

He sagged and panted for a few moments, then grinned. "Good girl. You're amazing. But..."

I raised both eyebrows at him. "But? But what?" I gave him a menacing smile, which he responded to with a chuckle.

"But now it's time to return the favour." He rose, pulled up his pants and helped me to my feet. He pressed me back against a tree—one which still looked healthy—and ran his hands over my breasts. His rough palms grazed my nipples. He gripped them between his thumbs and forefingers and pinched hard enough to hurt.

I moaned and kissed him, fierce and hungry. My tongue drove into his mouth like I wanted him to drive into me. I thrust a few times, then he slipped away.

He started to kiss and lick his way down my body, starting with my neck, my collar bones, my chest. He paused to savour each nipple, licking and sucking and biting.

My body begged for him, but he took his time.

He worked down, tickling my navel with the tip of his tongue, then helped me out of my pants and panties. He looked up at me and smiled, a boyish, carefree look that almost made me forget what was at stake if we failed.

He crouched down lower and squeezed my ass, then pushed my thighs apart. I raised one foot and pressed it to the trunk behind me, opening myself up to him.

He ran a finger from my navel down over my pussy, to the folds and entrance. He rubbed lightly over my clit, barely more than a feather-like touch.

I pushed myself forward. "Please."

He rubbed two fingers over my pussy and massaged my clit.

I bit my lip to hold back a moan.

He slid a finger inside me, then another and bent to taste me with the tip of his tongue.

"So sweet," he murmured.

"I try," I said with a husky laugh.

He smiled up at me and kept my gaze as he licked me again, slower and deeper this time. His fingers stroked me inside, seeking and finding my g-spot.

I whimpered. My hips bucked with each lap of his tongue, each stroke of his fingers. Pleasure rose, hard and fast.

He worked me firmly with his mouth, teasing my folds and lightly running his tip over my clit.

My whole body ached so hard with desire I thought I might explode. I drew in my lower lip and chewed to keep from screaming out his name. My breath came out in ragged pants.

Gods. Gods' gods!

Every touch felt so good. I never wanted it to end. I tried to slow my rising desire, but nothing would suppress it.

"Please let me come," I whispered.

"Come," he said, his voice muffled by my pussy.

With a rush, my orgasm roared through me like the tide: strong, hard, unstoppable. Hot blood pounded through my ears, blocking out all sound but the moan which slipped from between my lips. That was followed by a sigh and my whole body sagged.

Huon caught me before I could fall, and lowered

me onto his lap. I nestled into him while my heart slowed back to its normal rate. He wrapped his arms around me and kissed my brow.

"I've been thinking," he said softly.

"That's always dangerous," I teased.

"It often is," he agreed cheerfully, "but this time it might prevent danger. To you."

I pulled back and frowned at him. "What are you saying?"

"I was thinking you should go back to the capitol. Mother could show you where the secret library is—"

"I'm not going back there to hide," I said, angry he'd even suggest something like that.

"I didn't mean for you to hide. If you could look through whatever is in there, you might find something Birch missed."

"He wouldn't have missed anything," I replied. "He was meticulous."

"Maybe, but he didn't know about the keys. If there's one hidden there—"

"Then we'll find it after we find the key in troll territory," I said firmly. "We'll find them all together." Deep down, I knew he was right. If we had a head start on that key, we could find two at once. Waiting might waste time, but my pride wouldn't allow me to back down now.

"The more of us there are, the easier it should be to deal with screamspinners," I pointed out, more weakly than intended.

"I suppose that's true." He drew me back to him. "Although I suspect there will be more to this than just screamspinners."

"Like what?" I asked.

He hesitated. "I don't know," he said finally. "I think we should watch ourselves. Are you sure you won't reconsider going home?" He sounded hopeful, but with an undertone which suggested he knew what my answer would be.

"I'm sure," I said firmly. "But we should both try to go back to sleep." I didn't try to suppress a yawn. I was sleepy after our activities.

"That sounds like a good idea. Have you got room under that blanket?"

"I think I can share." I rose and started pulling my clothes back on.

"I like sharing," he said. He handed me my panties and watched as I pulled them on without falling over.

"That's fortunate." I found the blanket and swung

it around us both for the walk back to camp. "There's plenty of warmth for everyone."

He laughed, soft and low. "The perfect arrangement."

I smiled and pulled him down into the spot where I had been sleeping beside the fire. Saff and Fletcher were both snoring now, and Kale seemed to be dreaming.

Huon was right, it was the perfect arrangement.

CHAPTER SEVENTEEN

"*A*re you sure this is the way?" Huon asked.

Tavar turned and gave him a dark look.

"Maybe you should stop asking that every five minutes?" Saff suggested.

"That was not five minutes," Huon protested.

"More like three," I teased.

Huon spluttered in protest, but his eyes shone with humour. "It was at least ten."

"It was eight and a half." Fletcher held up his wrist. He wore a watch with a black band and silver arms ticking around the white face. "I was timing it."

"You too hmmm?" Huon nodded toward Fletcher. "As king of the Fae, I could have you executed." A smile tugged at the corners of his mouth.

"Not if you like your balls intact." I stepped past him and followed Tavar, who had resumed walking.

"I do, rather," he admitted. "But you like them too much to damage them."

"Interesting theory," I said over my shoulder.

"Summer isn't lacking in balls," Saff pointed out. "Hers or ours."

I chuckled. "He's right, you know."

"Of course I am," Saff replied.

"Are they always like this?" Fletcher asked Kale.

Kale cocked his head and looked from one to the other of us. "As far as I can tell, yes, they are. I think it's their way of relieving the tension."

"Ahhh, I see." Fletcher nodded. "That makes sense." To me he said, "At least Huon isn't asking if we're there yet."

"That was going to be my next question," Huon said. "And that's King Huon to you."

Fletcher flushed and opened his mouth.

Before he could say anything, I socked Huon lightly on the chest. "No one calls him that."

"That's because no one has any respect for me." Huon mock pouted.

I laughed. "Poor baby."

"See?" he said to no one in particular.

Fletcher smiled, then fell into step beside me. "Wouldn't it be easier to fly?"

I shrugged. "Tavar refused to let us fly her."

"I also object to flying, if anyone cares," Khat remarked.

"Too scary?" A smile tugged at the corners of my mouth.

"Certainly not!" He sounded affronted. "I simply like my feet on the ground. Also, I get sick from the motion."

"Ah." Well, no one wanted to get covered in mimicat vomit.

"Maybe Tavar could draw a map and she and the cat could catch up later." Fletcher looked nervous every time Khat spoke. Given the lack of talking cats in the human realm, it wasn't surprising, but surely it wasn't the strangest thing he'd seen in the Fae realm?

I eyed him for a moment. "You must be eager to get home?"

He nodded and stepped over a fallen log before he said, "In a way I am. I should check on my house-plants." He averted his gaze.

"There must be someone there who misses you," I said gently. "You mentioned a brother?"

"He probably hasn't noticed I've gone," he replied.

"Well, that's true." I ducked under a particularly brown set of leaves.

Fletcher looked at me in surprise. "Um, thanks." He flushed.

I blinked. "Oh! I just meant because time passes more slowly there than here. You've likely only been gone for a day or two."

His mouth formed an O. "Really? I didn't know that."

"Really," I said firmly.

"People might wonder about the beard." He rubbed his chin. "I kind of like it."

"Me too," I replied. "Fae men don't usually grow them. Well, maybe those over the age of two hundred."

"How old are you?" he blurted, then flushed again. "I'm sorry, I know it's rude to ask."

"It is?" I cocked my head at him. "That must be a human thing. We don't care too much here. I'm a hundred and twenty-three."

His draw dropped. "Wow. You must have seen a lot."

I shrugged. "I suppose so, but I'm barely an adult in Fae terms. Saff and Huon too, that's why they act like children." I grinned as Saff turned and poked his tongue out at me.

"See what I mean?" I poked my tongue out in return.

Fletcher chuckled. "You do all seem about the same age as me. I suppose age is just a number."

"Right." A shiver passed through me and I stopped. "What was that?"

"What was—" Fletcher shuddered. "Oh." He looked disturbed. "I felt like an icy breeze went through my blood."

"How could a breeze—" Huon also stopped and looked at us in confusion. Then he too shuddered. "All right, I get it now. What the fuck?"

All eyes turned to Tavar. I hoped to see her unconcerned, but she looked troubled. She swallowed visibly.

"They say the souls of the trullen guard the key," she said.

"It would have been nice to know that in advance," Huon pointed out.

"Indeed," Kale agreed. "Will they let Fae pass through unharmed?

"They'll have to," I said and resumed walking. "We have to get the key."

Tavar nodded. "They may allow it. They may not. It will depend on the task they've been given."

"Task?" I asked.

She nodded, but didn't elaborate. "The cave is close."

Her words were punctuated by a scream which shattered the peace of the forest. Every winged insect and bird in the area took flight, clicking and squawking in protest.

I jumped, my hand pressed to my racing heart.

"Screamspinners," Kale remarked.

I nodded. Of course it was. We had expected them, but hearing them was another thing, especially so suddenly.

Another scream rent the air, this time from another direction. Another sounded a moment later, from close behind us.

My heart hammered, eyes swivelled back and forth, trying to find the creatures amongst the lower hanging branches.

Yet another scream came from near the last one.

"They're herding us," Fletcher said. His face was pale.

My mouth went dry. "You're right."

"Just a wild guess here," Saff said, "but we shouldn't go in the direction they want us to go. Right?"

Tavar rubbed her earlobe thoughtfully. "It is the direction of the cave."

"Maybe it's not the cave we're supposed to go to?" Kale suggested. Even he looked rattled by the screamspinners.

"What do you mean?" Huon asked.

"The key might be near the cave, rather than in it," Kale said evenly.

"The legend says—" Tavar started.

"Legends have been wrong before," Kale said. "There may not even be a key. Or a cave."

"There *has* to be a cave. The mimicat council has passed the information down for generations." Khat's tail whipped back and forth in agitation.

"It might be a metaphorical cave." Kale pinched his lower lip between his thumb and forefinger.

"How can a cave be metaphorical?" Khat seemed particularly agitated that anyone would question the integrity of mimicats in general, and him in particular.

"Caves are dark," Fletcher said, as though speaking to himself. "Enclosed. The sides press down on you. You're alone and you feel like you'll never see the sun again..."

I stepped over and put my arms around him. I spoke softly in his ear. "It's all right, you're not in there anymore. We got out, remember?"

He blinked. "Right," he said slowly. "Sorry, I just—"

"It's fine," I assured him. "You went through a lot. No one expects you to get over it straight away."

"I don't suppose you have any shrinks in the Fae world?"

I gave him a blank look.

"I guess not." He sighed.

I kissed him on the cheek and stepped back, but kept an arm around his shoulder. "I guess that answers the question. A cave *could* be a state of mind."

"I once read one of the books in Birch's library," Huon said slowly. "The secret library." He shot me an apologetic look. "Our people used to do mind exercises to relax. Apparently some would go into a kind of spirit world."

"They would meditate and hallucinate?" Fletcher asked.

"What if they weren't hallucinating?" Huon asked. "But actually seeing—something. A glimpse into another world, or..."

"Or a cave," I finished for him. "Tavar, did the legends mention anything about that?"

She shrugged. "The legends are vague at best.

They mention this spot and a vault. We have always assumed it was a cave."

Khat paced in front of us, back and forth. "Our stories tell of a place of darkness, fright and endless screams. Only the bravest may enter... Blah, blah blah. And they need magic to do it, but mimicat magic isn't enough. That sounds like a cave full of screamspinners to me."

"Endless screams? What fun," Saff said ironically, a nervous smile on his full lips.

"Only if you have a twisted idea of fun." I chewed my lip for a moment and thought.

"We can hear the screams from here." I flinched as another one filled the air. "And the souls, or whatever made us shiver, are frightful."

"And we're brave," Huon pointed out.

"Speak for yourself." Saff's head jerked around at the sound of another scream.

"I was." Huon patted him on the shoulder and made him jump.

"Gods, what the hells?" Saff turned to glare at him. When Huon only grinned in reply, he made a rude gesture with his finger.

Kale cleared his throat. "We certainly have magic."

"Maybe I'm supposed to blow a hole in the side of

the mountain," I said dryly. "But I think we should try this meditation thing first." I tapped my finger against my lip. "Huon, what else did the book say?"

He mimicked my gesture, either accidentally or to be facetious—I suspected the former—and looked thoughtful. "It said something about sitting comfortably and letting the mind wander. I suppose those with the right magic could see into… wherever."

"How are we supposed to get a key from, 'wherever,' though?" Saff asked.

Silence fell amongst us for a few moments, broken only by screams which seemed more distant now.

"I suppose we'll have to try and see what happens," I said.

I lowered myself to the ground and placed my bag beside me.

"All of us?" Fletcher sat, but his eyes were wide.

"No," Huon said firmly. "You, Saff, Tavar and Khat, keep watch. It might be that none of us can do this, but I want you four guarding us if we can."

Fletcher and Saff both looked relieved. Tavar nodded and remained standing. Khat plopped down and started to lick his butt.

Kale sat next to me and took my hand. When I looked questioningly at him, he said, "If we do this mind wandering to, 'wherever,' we may be safer if we're not alone."

I nodded and reached out to Huon. Both their hands were warm and reassuring. If we sat like that for a while, and nothing happened, they gave me comfort against the screamspinners and whatever else might be out there.

I closed my eyes, tried to relax. For a long time, all I wanted to do was fidget, to open my eyes and see what the others were doing. I focused on my breathing and shut out the sounds of the forest, and Khat's tongue on his fur.

I exhaled through pursed lips. Just as I began to inhale, icy fingers grabbed me and I was tugged hard into darkness.

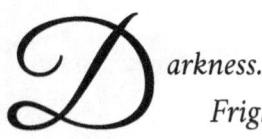 *arkness.*

Fright.

Endless screams.

Where the gods am I?

I blinked and squinted, trying to force something to appear in front of me.

Anything.

Nothing stretched out in front of me but blackness, unbroken, unrelenting.

At least the screams were muffled. Not scream-spinners, but something else. Fae, trolls, maybe humans.

"The souls of the dead." A voice spoke from beside me and made me jump.

"Kale?" I gradually became aware of his hand still laced in mine. My other still gripped Huon's.

"Summer?" Huon's voice was punctuated by a sudden burst of light. He held his hand in front of his face. Magic lit his mouth, nose and the bottom of his eyes.

"I'm here. I can't light anything unless I let go of your hands." I was reluctant to do that, in case I lost them again.

"One of us needs to try." Kale illuminated his own face, then stepped away from me.

I felt his hand slide free and held back a gasp. I half expected him to disappear.

"Can you still see me?" he asked. He held his hand higher so I could see his mouth. The tug at the sides of his lips reassured me.

"Yes." Relieved, I used my own magic and glanced around. "Where are we? We're not dead, right? Ouch!" My arm hurt where Huon pinched me.

"No, not dead." In the light of his magic, the smile he gave me looked sinister.

"Not yet," I grumbled. "Do that again and I might reconsider though."

He laughed. "Promises, promises."

"That was more of a threat than a promise." I

took a few steps, my hand out. "So we're not dead. What was it that pulled us in here?"

"What do you mean?" Huon sounded genuinely confused.

"You didn't feel hands on your shoulders? They felt like cold fingers. Or the souls Tavar mentioned."

"I didn't feel a thing, did you, Kale?"

"Just Summer's hand. She pulled me off my feet. Or so it felt."

"That's Summer, always sweeping men off their feet," Huon joked. "Is anyone else here?"

No answer.

"I guess it's just us three, and whoever is screaming." I took a step and crunched something under my boot. A beetle. The same kind which attacked Fletcher and me, a blood beetle.

"Revenge is a bitch," I muttered. "So do we walk toward the screams or run like hells?"

"That depends," Huon said slowly. "Is this a real place or something in Summer's head?"

"Or something in between," Kale remarked. He sounded fascinated. "This could be some kind of netherrealm accessed via her mind."

"What does that even mean?" I asked.

"It means you may be able to manipulate it with your thoughts."

"In that case..." I thought about light and a key dangling right in front of us.

With a whoosh, a series of sconces burst into flame, illuminating walls and the floor.

We stood in a long, wide corridor, lined with dressed stone. The floor was teeming with beetles. They crawled along the tiled surface and clicked in fury at the sudden brightness.

I let out a squeak and magic shot out of my hand. It incinerated the creatures and sent shards of stone flying. I threw a hand over my eyes. Several small pieces struck my skin, but mostly it was a burst of dust.

"Shit, sorry!"

I slowly lowered my hand. Both men were shaking stone dust from their hands and wiping their faces. Their hair was coated in a layer of it.

Oops.

"It's all right. At least we can see now." Huon wiped dust from his eyes.

"No key though," I said. "I should have known it wouldn't be *that* easy." It was worth a try. "What now?"

Kale tapped his nose with his knuckle. "I think we need to walk toward the screams."

"Of course," Huon replied. "What could go

wrong?"

"Do you have a better idea, your highness?" Kale asked, no hint of mockery in his tone.

"Actually… no. If this is all in Summer's head, we can't die, right?"

"I wouldn't make that assumption," Kale replied. "We may be in her imagination and we may have actually passed through some sort of portal."

Huon looked thoughtful. "The second one seems more likely."

"What makes you say that?" Kale asked.

Huon grinned. "Because we're both dressed."

I swatted him on the arm.

"Ouch." He pulled his arm back. "I'm real at least."

"For now," I said. "Don't push your luck too far though."

"Why are you all always so loud?" Khat appeared in front of me. One moment there was nothing there but dead beetles. The next, the mimicat stood, tail swishing, eyes shining in the torchlight.

"What the hells? Where did you come from?" I looked at him sideways.

"I got bored, so I put my paw on you and here I am." He trod over the carcasses of several beetles and hissed. "I hate bugs."

"Can you take your paw off her?" Kale asked.

"Why would I want to?" Khat asked. "You clearly need my help."

"That's debatable, but now you're here, you might as well stay." I started down the corridor in the direction of the screams, although my skin was crawling.

"That's good, because I don't seem to be able to remove my paw anyway." He slunk along beside me, Kale and Huon close behind.

"How the hells are we going to get out of here?" Huon asked. "If we can't find the key, we might be stuck in here forever."

"I'm sure Saff and Fletcher will pull you guys out long before forever happens," I said. That left the question of how I would get out, but I'd worry about that later.

The screams grew louder with every step. The closer we got, the more I realised they weren't just screaming, they were pleading. They spoke in a language I didn't recognise, but I knew begging when I heard it. I did enough of it.

"Can anyone speak ancient troll?" I asked.

"Funnily enough, no," Huon replied.

"Neither can I," Kale said. "I suspect no one can. Even languages die eventually."

"They're asking to be released from eternal torment," Khat remarked.

I stopped to stare at him.

"What?" he asked. "Mimicats' affinity for languages doesn't stop at living ones. I told you we have magic of our own."

"Yes." I resumed walking. "Can you ask them where the key is?"

We stepped out into a massive chamber. A huge pool stood in the centre, ringed by flaming torches.

"That's not water," Huon said nervously. He pointed toward the pool.

Within the stone edges, shapes swirled, opaque and frantic. I saw an arm here, a head there. A ghostly foot protruded before it disappeared again.

"Souls," I said softly. "We're supposed to let them out of there?"

"That's what they're asking for," Khat replied.

"That doesn't mean it's a good idea," Huon pointed out. He stepped closer to the pool. Several arms reached out toward him before they disappeared again.

I pressed a finger to my lips and looked around for any sign of a key. The pool was the only thing in the chamber and there was no corridor past it. If the key was anywhere, it would be in here.

"Can you ask them if it's in there?" I lowered my hand and gestured toward the pool.

Khat kept his distance, but spoke in words which sounded strange to my ears, as though Fae and troll were mashed into one.

The souls stilled and fell quiet. A face emerged, just eyes at first, then nose and mouth. Male or female, I couldn't tell, but it looked more troll than Fae.

They spoke.

Khat translated. "They say they are the guardians of the key. They gave their souls to rid the realm of dark magic."

"Tell them the realm is dying. Dark magic is holding lesser magic captive and i we don't free it, we'll all die."

Khat spoke to the soul. "They say it was foretold that one would come to seek the key to save the world. They do blather on, don't they? I'll ask if they can give us the key or not."

"So much for diplomacy," Huon muttered. "Khat, don't offend them."

Khat turned toward Huon and looked affronted. "Of *course* not. I'm the epitome of good manners."

Huon snorted. "Right."

"Go on, Khat," I said. I wanted to be away from this place. It gave me the creeps.

"Thank you." He turned back to the pool and spoke. His tail swished at the response the soul gave.

"What is it?" Huon asked.

"They said they can only give the key to the fore-told and only after they are released. They want to speak directly to the foretold so they can discern if the threat to the realm is real."

I stepped forward.

"Not you," Khat replied. He raised a paw and pointed toward Kale. "Him."

Kale's eyebrows shot up to his hairline. "Me? Why would *I* be important?"

"I was wondering the same thing," Khat said dryly.

"Can you ask them?" Kale asked. He actually looked rattled.

Khat sighed and spoke again to the soul. "They don't know. Only that you're the one they need to speak to."

The dark skinned Fae ran a hand over his hair. "I suppose I must speak to them then."

"Are you sure?" I asked. "We have no idea what might happen to you if you do." I put a hand on his arm. "I'd hate if anything bad happened to you."

"I would also hate that," he said, with no hint of humour on his face in spite of his words. He faced me and put an arm around me to draw me closer. "I care about you," he said softly.

"I care about you too," I replied.

"When this is over," he jerked his head toward the pool, "I would like to see where this can go. I don't mind if it's messy."

I blinked back tears and smiled. "I'd like that."

He leaned in and pressed his lips to mine, just lightly.

Khat coughed. "I could be wrong, but I think being in a place full of souls for too long might end badly. Can we hurry this up a bit?"

Kale pulled back and grimaced. "He's right. We'll have plenty of time later for this."

"I hope so," I replied. "I mean, of *course* we will."

He nodded and gave me another quick kiss, then stepped away, toward the pool.

"What do I need to do?" he asked.

Khat spoke to the soul again. "Kneel down beside them."

Kale knelt. The soul raised ghostly hands and pressed them to the side's of Kale's head. The moment they touched, Kale began to howl in agony.

I started forward, but Huon grabbed my arm and held me back.

"There's nothing you can do," he said.

"But we can't just stand by…" Tears slid down my cheeks. "There must be something." Short of trying to blow the pool to smithereens, I had no idea.

My vision blurred, but Kale was clear in my ears. His screams seemed to go on for hours, shredding every last nerve in my body.

I raised my hand to—I don't even know what. I threw my head back, ready to scream too, when the chamber fell silent.

Kale dropped to his knees, hands on either side of his head.

Huon let me go and I rushed forward to gather Kale in my arms.

"Oh gods, gods, fucking gods, Kale!"

Blood trickled from his eyes and ears, his breathing was shallow, but he was alive.

"Summer," he rasped. His voice sounded ruined.

"The souls said you were telling the truth," Khat said helpfully.

"No shit we were," I muttered. I reached into a pocket, pulled out a handkerchief and dabbed at Kale's face. "They better be handing over the fucking key."

"We have to free them," Kale said. Every word was forced and pained.

"How?" I asked. "Did they tell you or just torture you?"

Kale made a sound between a laugh and a cough. "I saw a hundred lifetimes. All locked in here to keep us safe. They've been in limbo for a thousand years. It's past time they moved on."

"Yes, but *how*?" Huon asked, as impatient as I was.

Kale hesitated.

"Don't tell me one of us has to stay here so they can be free?" I demanded.

"No, but their release might let a bit of dark magic back in the world," Kale said. "It will make the realm deteriorate faster."

"Shit," I said under my breath. "What choice do we have?" I looked from him to Huon, then to Khat.

"None I can see," Kale said softly. "We may only have days to find the second and third keys."

CHAPTER NINETEEN

Kale's words echoed in my ears.

"We better work fast then," Huon said. "Now, how do we free these souls?"

Kale explained.

I grimaced, but took his hand and Huon's.

"I'll sit this one out," Khat remarked. He flopped down near a torch and started to roll on the ground, tail waving in the air.

"Well if you *want* to get covered in beetle shells." I grimaced at him and then shrugged. Mimicats were strange creatures.

Kale reached out a hand to the soul. They grabbed his arm and seemed to pass right through him. They slid from his hand to mine.

The moment they touched me, I felt like my

blood ran cold. I tried to scream, but no sound came out. Then they were gone, into Huon.

He groaned and muttered something I couldn't make out. It sounded like a swear word. I watched the soul ripple across him to his far hand, shoot out and disappear into the air.

"That was easy," I said, although I wanted to throw up my last meal.

"That was only the first one," Kale said as another soul rose and slid through him.

"How many?" Huon asked through gritted teeth.

"I don't know," Kale replied. "A few... hundred."

"A few—" Huon sounded like he was choking.

"Close your eyes and think about lesser magic," I suggested.

"I can think of at least a hundred things I would rather be doing right now," Huon replied, "and they all involve you, naked."

"Whatever it takes to get your mind off... ugh, two at once?" I shivered.

"They're coming quicker," Kale said, his voice higher.

He was right. The souls were moving in a blur now, passing so fast I couldn't discern one from another. I felt as though I was in a constant state of cold, with liquid ice wriggling through my bloodstream.

"I think there's only a few more." Kale's voice sounded strange.

"What about the key?" I forced out the words.

"I don't—here's the last few."

I hoped so, my teeth started to chatter. I looked toward the pool. It was empty now. The last soul slid into Kale, then over into me. Here, it stopped.

"What the..." My stomach heaved.

My vision blurred and I felt faint. My head began to ache, as though the soul was trying to work its way inside. I saw a lifetime flash before me. One which wasn't mine. A woman, a trullen, born without wings, her life a series of agony and ridicule. Outcast from her own people, even though she lived amongst them. She gave her soul to save the very people who taunted her.

Don't let my sacrifice be made in vain.

With that, she fled my body, passed through Huon's and was free.

I sagged and almost fell as Kale and Huon did the same. I stood there for a moment, then let them go, fled a few steps away and heaved out everything in my stomach onto the floor.

From the sound of it, both guys were doing the same thing.

"When you have a minute," Khat said after a few moments.

"What?" Huon spat on the floor and wiped his mouth.

Khat pointed toward the pool with his paw. Instead of ghosts, there lay a single, silver key in the centre.

Where before I had assumed the pool was deep, I saw the bottom, not even a metre below. All those souls; it must have been a tight fit.

"It looks a little small," I remarked. "Is that the right key?"

"What else could it be?" Huon asked.

"I'm certain we'll know when the time comes," Kale said.

"I suppose so," I conceded. "Are you going to pick it up? You are the foretold, right?"

He licked his lips. "Apparently." He frowned so a deep crease appeared in his forehead.

"We could hold onto you?" I suggested. "In case that's deeper than it looks." Or was another trap door.

"That might be best," he agreed.

Again, we held on to each other and Kale stepped toward the lip of the pool. He put out a hand as though checking for a barrier of some kind. Evidently, he didn't find one, as he stepped into the pool.

I held my breath, sure he was about to be dragged away.

He leaned down, drawing me over with him. Huon held me hard before I fell.

"Just a bit closer," Kale said to himself. "Almost." He crouched and grabbed up the key.

The moment he did, the ceiling above us split in two and started to rain rocks down onto us.

"Now would be a good time to get us out of here!" Huon shouted.

"I don't know how!" I shouted back.

"Think of us being gone from here," Kale suggested. He leapt out of the pool.

"I—" A chunk of rock narrowly missed my head.

All right, brain, get us the fuck out of here.

I closed my eyes and focused. I pictured us back in camp, Fletcher, Saff and Tavar nearby.

The ground shook beneath our feet.

"Hurry up!" Khat hissed.

"What do you think I'm doing?" I asked between clenched teeth. "It's not working!"

"Maybe if we go back the way we came?" Huon suggested.

"It's better than standing here." I followed him back toward the corridor we were in when we first arrived.

Chunks of rock littered the floor. More pieces were falling. A stone the size of my head missed Huon by a hair.

"Fuck." He ducked sideways and almost tripped.

"Keep running!" Kale shouted from behind me.

Just as he said that, the ceiling of the chamber collapsed. It sent a wave of dust and tremors in its wake.

"We have to outrun it," Kale said. "If we can't pop out how we came in, we'll find another way."

I squealed as the floor rose underneath me, then slammed back down. I went flying and hit the wall so hard it left me stunned for a few moments,

"Summer, you need to get up." Huon grabbed my hand and pulled me to my feet.

I staggered a few steps before I fell to my knees. My head spun and everything hurt. "Get the key out of here!"

Huon skidded to a stop and waved for Kale to keep going. He scooped me up in his arms and ran, zigging and zagging around piles of rocks which were increasing in size by the moment.

"You should save yourself." I blinked away the grit from my eyes.

"I am," he replied. "I'm just taking you with me."

"Hurry up, or I'll bite you all," Khat said. He streaked past us.

"How would that help?" I asked, but got no response.

We reached the place we came in. Kale was waiting for us.

"I would suggest we join hands again, but we have very little time." Kale's words were punctuated by the collapse of the tunnel right behind us.

I grabbed onto him and Khat pressed himself against Huon's legs.

Nothing happened.

The tunnel rumbled and shook. Slowly at first, then with more force.

"We need to keep running." Huon did just that, but his expression was strained.

"I can walk by myself," I said. "Or better yet, fly."

Huon shook his head. "There's too much risk of your wings being hit. Don't worry, I've got you."

"You lot are too slow." Khat raced ahead of us and disappeared from view amongst the dust.

"It's nice to know he has our back," Huon said dryly.

"Perhaps he can lead the way," Kale said. He was panting. Sweat made rivers in the dust on his dark face.

"Or not." Huon nodded as Khat appeared in front of us.

"It's a dead end." The mimicat sounded disgusted. "We're all going to die!"

"That's an encouraging thought," I said dryly. "Maybe we can reach the others on the outside somehow."

"How?" Huon asked.

"I don't know... Maybe if we all think at one of them hard enough, they'll hear it." It was worth a try anyway.

Kale nodded slowly. "Let us try to reach Saff. We all know him better than the other two."

"Agreed," Huon said.

"Don't send him dirty thoughts," I said.

Huon smiled. "What makes you think I would do that?"

"I've met you," I said dryly.

"Have I mentioned *hurry up?*" Khat said frantically.

"All right, all right." I closed my eyes and thought

about Saff, telling him to let us out of here. I pictured him sitting on the ground beside us, watching us, moving closer to us…

"Oh!" Huon exclaimed.

My eyes shot open. "What?" To my bitter disappointment, we were still in the crumbling tunnel.

"Khat's gone," Huon said. "He was there and then he wasn't."

"Good, he can tell them to…"

Kale disappeared without a sound.

"Us next." I licked my lips and waited.

"Maybe I should put you…" Huon started to lower me to the ground when he too disappeared.

I fell the rest of the way with a painful thud.

"Well shit." I pushed myself to my feet and rubbed my ass.

"I guess no one else is holding my hand now," I said to myself. "Good, they're safe." I assumed they were anyway. At least they weren't here, in a tunnel on the verge of falling in on itself, and me.

I stopped and looked around. "How the hells do *I* get out of here then?"

The walls responded by shaking.

"Really? That wasn't the answer I was after." I rubbed my gritty face. "I could use a bath."

The walls shook harder.

"Yes, yes, I know. No bath for Summer. Maybe my sisters were right; I'm an idiot." I frowned. "I must be going crazy. I'm talking to myself and thinking my sisters were right about something."

I threw my head back and shouted, "They're the idiots!"

The shaking stopped for a moment, then resumed, twice as hard.

"Good job, Summer," I muttered. "All right, if I'm going to die, I might as well make it spectacular."

I drew in a breath and focused all my attention and magic at a section of wall. With everything in me, I sent the biggest blast of magic I had ever used, toward the stone.

The stone shattered into a thousand minute pieces.

For a while, I couldn't see past the dust. When it finally settled, I saw the hole I had made.

And the forest beyond it.

I took off at a sprint and threw myself through the hole just as the tunnel collapsed in on itself.

CHAPTER TWENTY

I hit the ground for the third time in a short while and cried out in pain.

Seriously, this was a habit I could live without.

I lay on the ground for a while, panting until I caught my breath. The air out here was fresh and smelled like wet dirt and trees. Better than dank stone and tired souls.

After a moment, I lifted my head and looked around. A scream echoed through the forest, but this time I didn't jump. Just another screamspinner.

That sound was soon followed by a different one, a shout.

"Summer!"

"Huon?" My own voice was little more than a squeak. I pulled myself to my feet and leaned against a tree. This close to the leaves, I smelled the taint of rot creeping in. The longer I stood there, the worse it got.

"Huon!" I called out louder. That blast of magic must have taken a lot out of me, I was exhausted. I doubted I'd be able to shout any louder if I had to.

"Summer!" He sounded closer now. Another voice joined the first. Then another.

Saff and Fletcher.

"Summer?" That was Kale. He sounded like he was only a few metres away.

"Kale, I'm over here." I blinked and struggled to keep my eyes open.

"Thank the gods." He caught me around the waist. "I've found her."

I sagged against him and closed my eyes.

"Where are you?"

"Oh."

"We need to lie her down."

I wasn't sure who spoke, but I felt a few tender hands on me. They helped me down, covered me with blankets. Someone held me close while shivers wracked my body.

"I think she's in shock. We need to keep her warm and comfortable. Here, put this under her head."

A warm hand lifted my head and a blanket was placed underneath me.

"Can you believe she blew a hole in the side of the mountain?" That was Saff. He sounded impressed.

"That *was* incredible," Kale agreed.

"That's our Summer." Huon sounded proud.

"She really is like no one else." Fletcher's voice was so close, he must be the one holding me.

"And you secured the key," Tavar stated.

"Yes," Kale replied. "Is it supposed to be this small?"

I couldn't make out her reply and their voices faded away.

"The key," I murmured.

"It's okay, Kale has it," Fletcher said. He stroked my hair lightly and kissed my cheek. "You did it."

"We all got out." I marvelled at that miracle.

"Yes. Saff said something about hearing you all yelling at him."

"That's right." I heard Saff and felt him flop down beside me. "Huon said, 'Help us, you fucking idiot,' so I knew it was him." He chuckled.

"That would be Huon," I muttered. "Always with the manners."

"Shhh, you should get some rest," Fletcher urged.

I nestled down into him, but I needed to know one more thing. "The souls said the realm would die faster."

They both hesitated. I cracked my eyes open to see them look at each other.

"The trees around us got brown just before you blew out the mountain," Saff admitted. "But you have time to rest. The realm won't end today."

That should have been reassuring, but the realm might end tomorrow instead. I couldn't help if I was exhausted, so I closed my eyes again and let sleep claim me.

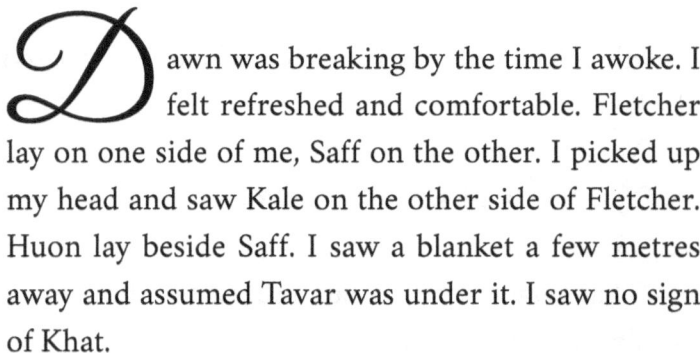

*D*awn was breaking by the time I awoke. I felt refreshed and comfortable. Fletcher lay on one side of me, Saff on the other. I picked up my head and saw Kale on the other side of Fletcher. Huon lay beside Saff. I saw a blanket a few metres away and assumed Tavar was under it. I saw no sign of Khat.

I stretched and Fletcher opened his eyes.

"Sorry, I didn't mean to wake you," I whispered.

"How are you feeling?" he mouthed.

"Much better," I mouthed back.

"Good." He gave me a soft smile and put an arm over me to draw me to him. "I was worried about you."

"I was worried about me too," I replied. I \expected to wake in pain, but I wasn't. Instead, I found my body responding to the way Fletcher looked at me. I scooted over and pressed my mouth to his.

He kissed me back, hungrily. His mouth opened and when my tongue slipped inside, he sucked on it as though he wanted to devour it.

I stifled a moan and slipped a leg over his. He pressed his body to me and I felt his cock harden against my leg.

I slid my hand down under the blanket and undid the front of his pants. His erection was hard and hot as I curled my fingers around it.

He groaned against my mouth.

Unable to wait, I undid my own pants and wriggled out of them, then tossed my panties aside with them. My leg still hooked over him, I pressed myself onto his cock, all the way down to his balls.

"Summer," he whispered. "Oh gods." He was still for a moment, then began to frantically thrust into me. His breaths were short, sharp grunts from between gritted teeth. His hand found my clit and started to rub with as much urgency as his cock was pounding into me.

I bucked my hips, matching him movement for movement, driving us both closer and closer to the edge.

I bit my lip as an orgasm washed over me, hard and fast like our coupling. I was still in the throes of pleasure when he gave a grunt and came, his release flooding inside me.

He thrust one more time, two more, then sagged.

"Wow," he sighed.

"I agree." I lay back and panted, enjoying how it felt to have his cock still resting inside me. "I hope we didn't wake anyone."

He chuckled low in his throat. "I'm certainly awake now." Reluctantly, he slid out of me and tucked the blanket back around us.

"Me too." I nestled down against him. "That was nice."

"It was. Maybe we can take our time next time."

"I'd like that." I especially liked that he wanted a next time. "Although quick and dirty is fun too."

"No argument from me," he replied. He exhaled softly into my hair. "I suppose we should get up and get food."

The reality of our situation crashed back into my

mind. I wished it could have stayed out for a while longer.

"I suppose so. And work out our next course of action." I reached around under the blankets for my clothes and pulled them on.

As I did up my pants, I rolled over and saw Saff peering at me, only his eyes visible above his blanket.

"Is it safe to come out now?" he asked.

"Why wouldn't it be safe?"

He jerked his head toward Fletcher. "I didn't want to disturb you." He lowered the blanket to reveal his smile.

I flushed. "You heard that?"

"Heard it, felt it, have a raging hard-on because of it." He looked pained, but grinned. "I think I better go off by myself for a couple of minutes."

I gave him a regretful look. "Sorry, we'll try to be quieter next time."

He pushed the blanket back and rose awkwardly. "Or you could invite me to join in, if you like."

"I'll bear that in mind," I said and watched him walk away, his gait exaggerated for my benefit.

"Oops," Fletcher said softly. "Hopefully he was the only one."

I waited, but no one else spoke up, so I stood and grabbed the shirt full of blackberries out of my bag. I tossed a berry to Fletcher and started nibbling on mine. By the time I finished and reached for another, Kale and Tavar were up and Huon was stirring.

Saff returned, looking relieved, and without a word we all sat down and exchanged looks.

I decided I may as well jump right in. I faced Tavar and spoke bluntly. "You said we might get into the human realm."

Fletcher twitched and looked at us both over his berry.

Tavar nodded. "It required a key, and for you to survive."

"Yes, well, I wouldn't expect to go anywhere if I was dead," I said dryly.

She regarded me, expressionless. "I imagine you wouldn't."

"Is this another legend which sends us off in the wrong direction?" Huon asked.

Tavar turned toward him slowly. "The first wasn't incorrect."

"Ultimately no," Huon agreed, "but it wasn't specific. We could as easily have searched for a literal cave while the realm died around us." He gestured toward the trees.

"It was in a literal cave," I pointed out. "Just one we couldn't have reached except the way we went in." I frowned. "I still haven't worked out how that happened."

"Your mind opened a portal," Tavar said. "A veil between here and inside the vault."

"But they were all still sitting in the same spot," Saff pointed out. "Only when we pulled them out did Summer disappear."

I blinked. "I did?"

Saff nodded. "When I took Huon's hand from yours, you were just—gone."

I shook my head slowly. "That's why you were calling out for me."

"You anchored the others there," Tavar said. "As soon as their connection to the anchor was gone, so were they."

"That makes sense," Kale said.

"I'm glad you think so." I snorted. I thought for a moment. "So I could have gone in alone and physically been there the entire time?"

"Possibly," she agreed. "I only know a small amount about this kind of magic. It's likely you couldn't have entered, or been allowed to live for long without the foretold being there with you."

I glanced at Kale. He looked embarrassed at being singled out.

I looked back to Tavar. "Did you know he was the

one they'd give the key to?"

"No. I've never heard of the foretold." Her lower lip twitched as though irritated at having not known every detail of our venture.

Huon flopped down beside me. "So you don't really know if we can get to the human realm or not?" he asked directly.

"I can make no guarantees," Tavar replied.

"So it's possible what we just did could have all been for nothing," he said. "Except to hasten the death of the realm."

Tavar bristled. "I didn't know it would have that effect.

"Didn't you?" he challenged. "Because it seems a bit too convenient to me."

"What are you saying?" I asked.

He regarded me through half lidded eyes. "I'm saying you could have died. So could Kale and I."

"Don't forget me," Khat said.

Huon waved a hand in his direction. "And the cat. Three Fae, including the Fae king, and a mimicat, all dead. All after having listened to a troll."

Tavar hissed. "The key was retrieved." She bared her teeth at him and her hand hovered near her knife.

"Yes, but what if we can't get another one?" he asked. "What if the key has no meaning at all?"

Silence fell for a long moment.

"I think it has meaning," I said softly. "I believe Tavar. I think she wants to help. If the realm dies, the trolls die too."

"Do they?" Huon asked. He looked around in challenge, but his eyes settled on Tavar.

"Yes, we do," Tavar said softly. "Our territory is dying faster than the Fae territories. Before long, we will have two choices: die or move into Fae lands." Before Huon could speak, she added, "Most would prefer to die first."

"That won't be necessary," I said firmly, "If the trolls need help, the Fae will give it. Right, *King* Huon?"

He frowned and shrugged. "I suppose so. We don't want to see anyone suffer."

I shook my head at his ungracious response, but I wouldn't push him any further.

"We can do this. We've shown that. We can find both of the other keys. We *will* find them."

"How?" Saff asked.

"The key will tell us," Kale said softly.

"It talks?" Saff asked in surprise.

Kale tilted his head and gave Saff a funny look.

"No. Ever since I touched it, it's been pulling me westward."

"Further west?" Huon groaned.

Tavar nodded eagerly, as excited as I'd ever seen her. "The legend says the keys are drawn together. If there's a way to retrieve the second, the key will show you the way."

"What about the third key?" Saff asked.

"Unless we find the second, then there will be no point in trying to find the third," I said.

My words were met with silence, punctuated by nods.

"She's right," Kale said.

"Of course, I'm always right," I joked, trying to lighten the mood.

Huon spluttered in laughter.

I stuck my finger up at him.

"Just think," Saff said to no one in particular, "the fate of the realm lies in their hands."

"We're doomed," Khat said. He put a paw over his eyes and rolled onto his back.

I shook my head at his melodrama, but grinned. "If anyone can do this, we can."

"Of *course* we can," Huon said.

If only we didn't have to venture deeper into the tainted parts of the realm to do it.

CHAPTER TWENTY-ONE

" So how does this work?" Kale and I walked a few paces ahead of the others. Him, because he had the key. Me, because I was curious, and hadn't had much time to speak to him.

"I don't know." He held the key on his dark palm and moved it back and forth slowly. "I feel it pulling me this way." He stepped past a pile of rocks which might not have been there the day before.

The damage I caused when I blew a hole in the base of the mountain was more obvious here. Rocks and scars tore up the ground. The bodies of dead beetles were scattered here or there, but not as many as I would have thought. Either they had disintegrated, or some other predator feasted on them.

I didn't want to think about the latter.

"I hope that isn't leading us astray," I remarked.

"As do I," he agreed. "I suspect not, but we should be on our guard."

"When are we not?" Saff asked from behind us.

"Most of the time," Khat said. "Your thoughts are more with your cock than your brain."

"How do you know what's going on inside my head?" Saff sounded more intrigued than annoyed.

"Lucky guess," Khat said.

Huon chuckled. "He gets you."

Khat regarded him. "You're just as bad. You all are. Except Tavar. Imagine that, a troll being the only sensible one."

She gave him a frown, then shook her head.

"See?" Khat said.

"Jealous?" Huon asked.

"Certainly not." Khat sniffed. "I have a perfectly good mimicat I hope to be reunited with very soon. If you would all focus and hurry up."

I glanced back toward Fletcher, who walked near the back of the group, silent and looking troubled. Everything I had seen and done in the last few days was strange. This must feel like a bad dream to him. The sooner we got him back to the human realm, the better for him.

The idea made my heart hurt, but it was his home

and if he chose to stay there, that would be his decision. Deep down, I hoped he'd come back with us, assuming we made it back. I wouldn't pressure him though. In spite of him talking about us fucking again, it wasn't that simple. Nothing was anymore.

"Hmmm, interesting." Kale's words drew my attention back to him.

"What is?" I asked. "Please don't tell me it's leading back into the vault?" I highly doubted there would be anything left of it anyway. If there was, it would be buried under the rubble.

"No," he replied. "It's tugging me southward."

I frowned. "South and west would take us around the mountains. There's nothing on the other side."

"How can there be nothing?" Fletcher asked, speaking for the first time in a long while.

"There's only ocean," Huon said. "Gods, I hope we're not supposed to go *under* the water."

I grimaced. "I doubt any of us are good enough swimmers."

"Are mermaids real?" Fletcher asked.

I stared at him. I was trying to think how to respond, when Khat laughed.

"Are you talking about Seafae?"

"I… maybe." Fletcher replied.

"There's no such thing," Khat told him.

"Oh," Fletcher's face fell.

"How would that help anyway?" Saff asked.

"I don't know," Fletcher admitted. "If the key was in the sea on Earth, I mean in the human realm, maybe they could go in and get it."

"A Seafae, if there was such a thing, wouldn't last an hour in the water in the human realm," Khat said scathingly.

"I guess so," Fletcher replied, his shoulders slumped.

"Is there a taint there too?" Saff asked, his head cocked to the side.

"Humans throw all their rubbish in the ocean," Khat said "it's their favourite way of getting rid of things."

Fletcher's eyes jerked up. "We're working on fixing it."

Khat sniffed. "So are we going to stand here and speculate, or are we going to keep walking?"

"This could take days," I said. "Unless we fly." I eyed Khat unapologetically. If he was going to blame Fletcher for his whole species' shortcomings, then he deserved a bit of discomfort.

"You could just keep walking," I told the mimicat. "I mean, we're only trying to reach the human realm."

He swished his tail and spoke in my voice, but with a mocking tone. "We're only trying to get to the human realm." He hissed and reverted to his own voice. "You know what's at stake, *Fae*."

I met his gaze, unwavering. "Flying it is then," I said. "Maybe you can shrink down a bit. I'm sure one of us has a pocket to spare."

He shot me a look of pure venom, then nodded toward Kale. "I'll travel with him. I know he won't eat me."

Kale arched an eyebrow, but said nothing.

"I bite," Khat reminded him. He scrunched up his face and shrank down small enough to fit in the palm of Kale's hand. "I'll ride on your shoulder." His voice was slightly higher now, in keeping with his size.

I bit back a laugh.

Kale scooped up the tiny mimicat and placed him on his own shoulder.

"Don't go digging your claws in," Saff said easily.

"I make no promises," Khat squeaked.

I stepped over to Fletcher. "Do you want to fly with me?"

He smiled faintly. "I'd love to. I don't bite." He cast a sidelong look at Khat.

"That's a shame," Saff said. He spread his wings and rolled his shoulders.

I shook my head at him and wrapped my arms around Fletcher. Before I could uncurl my wings, Huon cleared his throat.

"What about Tavar?"

The troll watched us, looking unimpressed.

"Can you carry her?" I asked Huon.

Both looked horrified.

"I'll go with him." Tavar pointed toward Saff, who looked surprised, but nodded.

"Fine with me." He curled an arm around her and pulled her close, her bared breasts to his chest. His eyes widened. "I have a spare shirt if you'd like? It might be cold up higher."

"I'm sure I'll be fine." If Tavar was bothered by his discomfort, she showed no sign.

"Um, all right." He spread his wings and followed Kale, who had leapt skyward.

"Hold on tight," I said to Fletcher.

"I know you won't drop me," he said, smiling. He leaned in to kiss my mouth, then braced himself.

"Mmmhmmm," I replied. "I'll try not to."

Before he could respond, I had us climbing into the sky and over the treetops. From up here, the extent of the taint was more obvious and shocking.

It stretched almost as far as I could see. The horizon showed a healthier shade of green, but below us was an endless canopy of brown.

"That doesn't look good," Fletcher said.

"No. it doesn't." I hovered over the scar in the base of the mountain and peered into the hole I made. Most of it looked to have collapsed back in on itself.

He looked down in the same direction. "Remind me not to upset you."

I laughed softly, little more than a rumble in my chest. "I'm sure there's nothing you could do which would make me do that to you." Although, only a few short days ago, I might have done the same to Huon and Saff. I had all but forgotten to be mad at them by now though. We had bigger problems to worry about.

"We should follow the others."

This would take a while. We had to cross the mountain, which meant flying higher, in thinner air. If Fletcher got too heavy, I could shrink him down and put him in my pocket, so at least I wouldn't tire too much from his weight.

"Summer, are the Fae the only things which fly in the Fae realm?"

"Why do you ask?"

"Because we seem to have company."

I turned just as a huge, winged form shot up from the trees and soared toward us. It screeched, an ear piercing sound which went right through me and made me wince.

I shook my head to clear it just as the bird lunged.

"Shit." I managed to duck fast enough to avoid having my head pecked off by the enormous beak.

"What the hell is that?" Fletcher asked.

I made a mental note to tell him about all the hells Fae believed in, and said, "It's a roc. Nasty creatures. Very aggressive and territorial, but they stick to their own area. We must have flown over its nest."

"That must have a bloody big nest," he said.

I snorted, but didn't respond. He certainly wasn't wrong.

I looked around frantically, both for the other Fae and for—

"Look out!" I swerved as the roc's mate came screaming out of the trees. It missed us by a feather. The wind from its passing sent my hair flying in every direction. I shook my head to get it out of my eyes.

"Can you blow them up?" Fletcher called out frantically.

"They're only protecting their babies." I needed to get us out of here, and quickly. I didn't want to deprive innocent birds of their parents, even if they were huge, scary and cranky.

"Summer!" Huon waved at me from twenty metres away. One of the rocs spotted him and veered away from me to go after the Fae king.

"Huon!"

Without thinking, I shrunk Fletcher so fast he almost slipped out of my grasp. He scrabbled to hang on to my shirt. Right before he fell, I grabbed onto him with one hand.

"Warn a guy next time," he said.

"Sorry. Um." I didn't have time to do anything else, so I shoved him down the front of my top.

His hands scrabbled before he grabbed onto the inside of my shirt. "There are worse places to be." He looked up at me and smiled, in spite of wide, scared eyes.

"Yeah, yeah, just hold on. *Ow, not there.*"

"Oops, sorry. Wow, your nipples are huge." He sounded awed.

"It's an illusion. Now be quiet and let me concentrate." I held him in place with one hand while I wove back and forth, trying to stay ahead of the roc. Judging by the plain brown plumage, this was Mama

Roc. Daddy Roc had a streak of green down his side and on his head. Right now that streak was headed for Huon.

Huon tucked back his wings and dropped so suddenly I thought he was injured. Then I saw him skim the canopy.

The male roc screeched in annoyance and soared over the top of him.

I sent a blast of magic in the direction of the roc, close enough to scare but not hit him. He squawked and broke off the pursuit.

In the meantime, Mama Roc zeroed in on me. She let out a furious screech so loud it tore through me and knocked me sideways.

I windmilled my spare arm and beat my wings in a desperate attempt to stay in the air.

Fletcher squeaked in fright and disappeared inside my shirt.

Lucky him; I wished I could hide too.

Instead, I twisted in mid-air and sent a warning shot of magic toward the giant bird.

"I don't want your babies, all right?" I shouted. "If you kill us, they might die too."

The roc apparently didn't speak Fae. She wheeled around and came back at me, but this time she had her mate with her.

"Shit."

"What?" Fletcher's face reappeared.

"Um, nothing," I lied. "Just hang on."

"Summer!" I saw Huon waving at me.

"Are you crazy?"

He must be; the rocs banked and went after him again. He dropped hard and disappeared amongst the trees.

The female roc screamed in frustration. The distraction gave me the time to follow Huon's example.

I wrinkled my nose and hovered amongst the rotted leaves in the canopy.

CHAPTER TWENTY-TWO

"*I* think they're gone."

I hadn't seen Huon coming until he spoke. I jumped and twisted in mid-air to face him.

"Did you drop Fletcher?" He looked toward the ground, a worried expression on his face.

"I'm right here." Fletcher popped up between my cleavage.

"Oh, there you are." Huon chuckled. "Aren't you lucky?"

"As amusing as this is," I waved my hand toward the nearest treetop, "have you seen this?"

Huon's face became more serious. "I had noticed, yes."

"Noticed what?" Fletcher asked.

Neither of us answered him.

"We should catch up to the others." I rose and hovered high enough to peek over the canopy. All I saw was empty sky. "Unless they're smart enough to lie in wait, then we should be clear."

I glanced down toward Fletcher. "It might be better if you stay that size, just in case." It was certainly easier to fly without his weight added to my own.

"Fine by me," he agreed. "As long as you hold on tight."

I nodded and curled my hand around him more firmly. "Let me know if I squeeze too hard."

"Yes, that could get messy." Huon's wings flitted lazily behind him as he mimed his face being squashed, eyeballs popping out of his head.

"Thanks buddy," Fletcher said dryly.

"You're welcome." Huon grinned. "Come on then, we're getting left behind."

Cautiously, we popped up out of the trees and headed in the direction we'd last seen Kale.

As it happened, he and Saff had seen the rocs and stopped to wait for the rest of us.

Tavar looked unimpressed, seated on a thick branch fifty or so metres above the ground. Khat must have curled up in Kale's pocket, or he would have been complaining loudly.

"The key is tugging harder," Kale said as he resumed his place in the lead. "I think we're close."

"Is it possible the key is really here?" I had to speak loudly to be heard over the rush of the wind.

"At this stage, I think anything is possible," Kale called back.

"I guess so," I said under my breath. I wouldn't be surprised by a thing I saw from this point on.

A glimmer of light caught my eye up ahead, a vast expanse of bluey-green. The tang of salty air made my nostrils flare to suck in more. Anything to alleviate the smell of dying foliage.

"The beach is up ahead," Kale called out.

"Thank the gods!" Saff replied. He looked strained from carrying Tavar, who looked as stiff as a board.

"Where? I love the beach." Fletcher thrust his head up higher and strained to see.

I laughed softly. "You'll see it soon enough, we're about to land." I turned to catch Huon's eye and he nodded. His face was red and he looked ready to burst. Containing himself had never been his strength.

Kale landed on a long, narrow expanse of beach near the base of the mountains. The rest of us followed suit, arrayed around him as if we'd silently agreed to protect the key-holder.

I hastily crouched to let Fletcher climb down and enlarged him to the same size as the rest of us.

I straightened as Huon stalked toward Tavar, who had barely stepped away from Saff.

"Why didn't you tell us?" Huon demanded.

I expected her to be confused, but she averted her eyes.

Saff, on the other hand, looked perplexed. "Tell you what?"

"Why don't you explain it?" Huon suggested, hands on his hips, eyes flashing with an anger I rarely saw. In other circumstances, it would have been as hot as all the hells.

Okay, it was still hot, but now really wasn't the time.

Tavar shrugged. "We were trying to find a solution ourselves," she said softly. "We didn't think we needed the Fae to intervene."

"Would someone please explain what the fuck you're talking about?" Saff demanded.

"The trees," I said, drawing all eyes toward me. "They've been dying for a long time. Maybe since we lost lesser magic. It's not a new thing." I fixed my eyes on Tavar's. "Is it?"

"No," she replied shortly. "It's not."

"And the trolls, in their wisdom, decided the Fae didn't need to know," Huon raged. "All the times that's been wasted—"

Tavar rounded on him. "Not wasted. We wouldn't have found the first key had we not spoken to the elders and learned all the lore surrounding lesser magic. We don't have books and libraries like the Fae do. Our knowledge is all here." She tapped the side of her head. "Legends, stories, knowledge, it's all passed down from one generation to the next, but we had to listen to it and decipher it as best we could."

"Maybe with our help—"

She interrupted Huon again. "The elders would not have spoken to you. If not for Korta agreeing to listen to you, the Fae would not be involved."

"Korta said we did this," I reminded her. "She blamed us for the taint."

"If the Fae hadn't cast out the trullen—"

Now it was my turn to interrupt. "Really? You're going on something which happened a thousand years ago? This is here and now."

Tavar sucked in a breath, then nodded. "The elders remind us of the past. I believe it is time to let it be left in the past. However, it is part of our lore and we will not stop speaking of it while trolls remain."

"That might not be much longer if we don't find these keys," Huon muttered.

She turned toward him slowly "Agreed. I don't think there is anything we could have gained by going to the Fae sooner. Would you have listened?" She raised her chin and stared Huon down.

"I..." He looked toward the ocean. The sun brought out the colour in his eyes and highlighted his long lashes. "I suppose we wouldn't, but if there's anything else you're keeping from us..."

"I must say the same to you," she replied. "I have told you all I know."

Huon nodded. "Us too." He glanced at me. I looked at Kale.

Kale nodded. "I've shared everything I'm aware of. We have nothing to gain from doing otherwise."

"I don't see any way to get back," Fletcher's voice broke through our tense conversation. He looked stricken.

"You were hoping for a door?" Saff asked, teasing gently.

"A door, a window... hell I'd settle for a cave full of those screaming spider-thingys." Fletcher kicked at the sand.

Saff stepped over to put a hand on his shoulder. "Hey, we'll help you get back home. All right? Huon, Summer and Kale will work something out."

"No pressure," I muttered. When Fletcher looked at me, I quickly added, "Of course we will. Kale, what is the key telling you?"

"Please say it's not guiding us into the water," Huon said.

Kale shook his head slowly. "No, it's not." He frowned. "I'm not sure what it's saying. It's not pulling, nor pushing. It's just... pulsing."

"What, like a heartbeat?" I asked.

"In a manner of speaking," he agreed.

"That's not unnerving at all," Saff said sarcastically. "It's not alive somehow?"

"Magic is a living thing," I reminded him. "Like plants and flowers are."

"None of those have heartbeats," Saff pointed out.

"Not that you can hear," I said.

The smile he gave me made my heart skip. I could easily fall for him. For all of these amazing guys. The strangest thing about it was that nothing about this felt strange at all. I cared about them and they all seemed to care about me. Apart from friendly jibes at each other, they all got along. That might be the most miraculous part of all.

"We should split up and look around," Huon said decisively. "Maybe we'll find a cave, or a door, or something."

"Maybe it's a magic portal like last time?" Saff suggested.

"The veil between worlds is a physical doorway," Kale reasoned. "Albeit a magical one. Not one accessed via the mind. In theory, anyone could pass through it. There's no reason to think this is any different."

"Except the veil is closed, as far as anyone truly knows." I looked at Tavar, who nodded.

"All the lore is vague on this matter," she replied. "Only that the key would lead the way. The assumption it leads to the human realm is only based on the knowledge of the key having been taken there and left."

"So it might have pulled us here to find a locked door," I said slowly. I wanted her to deny my assumption, but she nodded.

"It is possible."

"All right, I guess we do what Huon suggested and split up."

Fletcher hadn't moved far from me but he now stepped closer. "I'm with you."

"Me too." Saff moved to my side.

"I guess I'm with Kale," Huon said, unperturbed. "We'll go south. You head north."

"Me too." Khat stuck his head up out of Kale's pocket. He leapt out and promptly grew back to what I'd come to think of as his regular size.

Tavar looked thoughtful. "I will work alone and search along the base of the mountains. I'm better equipped for that terrain than the beach." She wrinkled her nose.

"You wouldn't want sunburnt breasts," Saff remarked helpfully.

Tavar blinked at him. "No, I would not." With a swing of her hips, she headed back inland.

"All right then, north it is," I said. The sun was only a couple of hands from the horizon. "We should meet back here before dark."

The others murmured their agreement and Saff, Fletcher and I started off up the beach.

"What do you think we're looking for?" Saff asked.

"A hidden immunity idol?" Fletcher suggested with a laugh.

"A what?" I turned to stare at him.

"It's… it's a human realm thing. I'll show you if we get there."

"All right then." I exchanged confused glances with Saff. He shrugged.

"Anyway, I don't know what we're looking for," I replied. "If there's even anything to find. The first key wasn't in a place we expected, so there's nothing to say a veil, or a sliver of veil, will look like what we're used to."

I ran a hand through my hair, tugged on the ends. "The veil is a doorway, with an arch. So maybe we're looking for an arch."

"If that's the case, wouldn't someone have noticed an archway on a beach before?" Fletcher asked.

"I don't know. Did anyone notice a trapdoor in the middle of a field before we did?" I asked.

"If they did, I didn't see them," Fletcher replied. "Maybe they were too sensible to touch it."

Perhaps I should have been offended at his suggestion that I wasn't sensible. I might have if it wasn't accurate. On the other hand, he touched it too, so...

"Who comes here though?" Saff reasoned. "This is troll territory and you saw how fast Tavar took off, away from the beach. There could be a whole lot of the gods know what that no one knows exists."

"I guess that's possible," I admitted. I puffed lightly as we climbed a dune and slithered down the other side. I narrowly avoided falling on my ass in the sand. Only windmilling my arms saved me, but my feet slipped deep under the soft grains.

"Quicksand is more or less a myth here too, isn't it?" Fletcher asked. "Sand that swallows up people."

"I didn't come all this way to die by being eaten by sand," Saff remarked.

"Me either," I pulled my feet free and stomped a few paces forward to the damp sand closer to the tide.

"Wait a minute." Fletcher caught my arm. "The tide wasn't that close a minute ago."

"The tide is coming in." Saff looked unconcerned.

"That fast though?" Fletcher pointed.

The tide rose several metres in the last few minutes. If it kept going, it would swallow up the beach in a matter of moments.

"We might have to spend the night on higher ground," I remarked. That didn't seem like a big deal to me. Why was Fletcher so worried?

"Did you see the high tide line?" Fletcher asked. "When we got here, it was halfway up the beach. It's past that already. The ocean doesn't usually behave like that. Not unless there's a storm or a tsunami."

My lips dropped apart. "Or dark magic," I whispered.

CHAPTER TWENTY-THREE

We moved off the beach and into the dunes and foothills beyond as the water rose. The beach was swamped in a matter of moments. The water churned like an angry beast. Waves seemed to reach for us, whitecaps in place of grabby fingers.

I had never heard water roar like it did now, thunderous crashes as it pounded onto the beach.

Saff and I stood with our wings outstretched, in case we needed to flee suddenly.

Fletcher stayed close to us both, his face pale, tight with anxiety.

"I haven't had much to do with oceans, but this is definitely strange." I almost had to shout up to be heard over the noise. "It feels as though it's alive somehow." I glanced sideways at Fletcher. "They don't do this in the human realm?"

"Not exactly, no. We get king tides and whatever, but I feel as though if I got too close, this would grab me and drag me under. It feels like it's... malevolent. Does that sound crazy?"

"Usually I would say yes, and make a joke about it," Saff said, "but this is..."

"Not funny?" I suggested.

"Right," he agreed. "Not at all amusing."

"Not a good way to get wet either," Fletcher said. He looked sidelong at me.

"Under the circumstances, I can only give that a two," I replied.

"That's fair." He nodded.

"I think so." I stepped back and crouched down to pick up a stick.

"What are you doing?" Saff asked, his upper body twisted to watch me.

I straightened up. "Just testing something out." I leaned forward and tossed the stick. It turned end over end and landed in the water. The waves growled louder, almost deafening, before the stick was sucked down and disappeared.

"That was—"

The water heaving interrupted whatever Fletcher

was about to say. A funnel formed in front of us, maybe a metre wide at the base and twice as high.

Before I could even throw my hands over my face, the stick rose to the surface and was spat back out toward me.

I ducked sideways. The stick narrowly missed striking the tip of one of my wings.

"What the fuck?" I shook my head and gaped. "All right, I *know* that's not normal ocean behaviour."

"Not really." Fletcher took my hand and tugged me back, away from the water. "It's getting closer. Maybe we should fly out of here. Get to higher ground."

"I think that's a good idea," I agreed.

"You don't think…" Saff looked back in the direction we'd come.

"What?" I prompted.

"Well, Tavar seemed in a hurry to get off the beach. Could she have known this would happen?"

"No," I said firmly. "I believe her when she says she's on our side." I put an arm around Fletcher and took off.

The water surged forward and almost splashed the bottom of my boots.

It washed over Saff's legs, drenching him to the knees. He let out a squeak and tried to jump up out of the way. The waves encased his legs and pulled him back, toward the open ocean.

"Saff!" I hovered just above the water. The waves rose like fingers reaching for me.

I was forced back, further inland.

"Summer!" Saff shouted. His face was pale, hand outstretched toward me. His wings beat furiously, but he was getting nowhere.

I looked around frantically. A few metres away stood a rocky outcrop. Was it far enough from the waves? It would have to do.

I flew toward it and all but dumped Fletcher on the top. He grunted and waved his arms to right himself.

"I'm fine," he said insistently. "Go."

I nodded and shot back to Saff. The waves dragged him further out, but he was still fighting to stay upright. His face was almost as red as his hair now, from the exertion.

"Saff, take my hand!" I shouted as I drew closer.

"It'll get you too!" he argued.

"No it won't." I wished I was as confident as I sounded.

I stretched out my hand. He was still two metres away.

One metre.

Half a metre.

He disappeared under the water.

"*Saff!*" I screamed so hard it made my throat raw.

I dove down closer to the waves, searching for him but seeing only white water, writhing and churning.

Then the ocean became dead calm. In a heartbeat it went from churning beast to as still as a lake.

"Saff?" I searched for him under the surface. I saw sand, fish, even a clump of seaweed.

I saw no sign of Saff.

I flew in a zigzag pattern back and forth across where I saw him last. Gradually, I flew further and further out, away from the shore. As the moments passed, I grew more and more frantic.

If I didn't find him quickly...

No, I couldn't think about that.

"Saff! *Saff!*" Despair began to wash over me, deeper than the waves. Tears trickled down my face and plopped into the ocean.

The moment they made contact, the seas churned again. It made a strange hiccuping sound and belched up a massive funnel of water. For a moment, I thought it would head toward me.

Instead, it leaned toward the shore, gave a heave and spat Saff out, metres above the ground. He flew like a rag doll and slammed into the sand as the tide retreated.

"Gods!" I flew toward him at the same time Fletcher jumped down from the rock and started to sprint.

We reached Saff at the same time and fell to our knees.

Saff's face was pale and still.

"Oh hells, is he…" I reached out a hand to touch his face. The moment my fingers connected, he rolled over and coughed out a lungful of sea water onto the sand.

"Oh, thank goodness." Fletcher put a hand on his back and patted lightly while Saff emptied his stomach.

I stroked Saff's forehead and kept his hair from getting in his way. "Are you all right?"

Saff spat. He groaned and slowly rolled onto his back. "Uh, I've felt better, but I'm still here. More or less."

The colour gradually returned to his face, but he lay for a long while with his eyes closed.

"I think all the necessary bits are there," I said lightly.

He half opened one eye, then felt around his groin. "Yes, that's still intact." His hand flopped back down.

"We should get off the beach," Fletcher said. "In case whatever that was decides to swallow us all up."

I murmured my agreement and offered Saff a hand. "Can you stand?"

"Anything to avoid going through that again," Saff said as he sat up. "She was strange."

I froze. "She?"

He blinked at me. "You didn't see her?"

"See who?" Fletcher asked.

"There was a—" Saff's face swung back toward the water. "You're right, we should get off this beach, then I'll tell you."

He pulled himself to his feet and stomped toward the dunes. He dripped with every step.

"You look like you need wringing out," I joked, trying to relieve some of the tension.

"I feel as though I've been wrung out already," he replied. He sounded more his old self, but his eyes kept darting back toward the tide.

We walked up a rise, well above the high tide line and flopped down amongst some twisted trees which still looked remarkably healthy.

"So, what did you see?" I asked.

Saff pulled off his shirt and hung it on a branch

beside him. His toned chest and stomach drew my eye and distracted me for a few moments.

I forced my eyes back to his face when he spoke.

"You know how we said Seafae aren't real?"

I nodded and gestured for him to continue.

"Well, I saw a woman under the water. At first I thought I was dead. Maybe I was." His brow creased. "She looked at me as though she could see right through me, into my soul." He shivered. "She had these huge eyes, the same colour as the ocean, but her hair was white. Like sand."

"Did she say anything?" I asked.

"Yes." Saff's expression glazed, lost in thought. "She said we need to solve the puzzle before we can pass through the veil."

"I knew we should have looked for an immunity idol," Fletcher muttered.

I gave him a confused look, then turned back to Saff. "What puzzle?"

He looked embarrassed, then said, "I have no idea. I wasn't exactly able to ask questions." He sucked in a breath and blew out through pursed lips.

I patted his muscular arm and gave him a smile. "It's all right, you're alive. That's what matters."

He gave me a wan smile. "I'm not so easy to kill, I guess."

"Or she didn't want you dead," I replied. "You did get spat out pretty hard."

"Don't remind me." He grimaced. "That was a lot of work to go to just to deliver a message. Couldn't she have just, I don't know, given us a wave and shouted out, "*Yoo-hoo*." He spoke in a high-pitched voice. "*I have to tell you something*. That would have gotten our attention."

I held back a laugh and rested the side of my head on my fingertips. "Yes, it would." I mulled it over for a few moments.

I couldn't discount the possibility Saff had hallucinated. Fae, in the sea, lying in wait? The idea was bizarre. Still, it wasn't even the strangest thing I'd heard that day.

"She gave no clue as to what she meant by a puzzle?" I asked.

Saff shook his head. "I assume that's what we're looking for here."

"It's not going to be something obvious," Fletcher reasoned.

I swung my head to look at him. "What makes you say that?"

"Firstly, if it was obvious, we would have seen it by now," he replied slowly. "Secondly, if it was easy to find, someone would have. If the idea was to keep people from finding the keys, then they aren't going to make it too easy."

"If she was Fae, and the loss of lesser magic is impacting her too, then what she did with Saff is probably all the help we can expect to get from her." I tapped my fingers against my cheek.

"Unless one of us goes back in," Saff remarked.

"No!" Fletcher and I said at the same time.

"Uh, all right then." Saff held up his hands at the forcefulness of our response. "It was just a thought."

"Yes, well, put it out of your head," I told him.

"I'm all for putting out." He batted his eyelashes and smiled sweetly.

Fletcher glanced at me. "What do you think? Maybe a four?"

I nodded slowly. "We should give him an extra point for almost drowning."

"Hmmm, good idea," Fletcher nodded. "Five it is then."

"I'm pretty sure that innuendo was worth a seven." Saff pretended to huff.

"Awww." Fletcher slapped his shoulder companionably. "It could have been worse."

Saff responded by giving Fletcher a smile so warm it sent my mind off in all sorts of directions, imagining them touching each other, their mouths…

I cleared my throat. "We should get back to the others. We'll have to look for this puzzle tomorrow." I hated to give up, even for a few hours, but after almost dying, Saff needed to rest and Huon and Kale would worry if we didn't get back in time.

"Maybe they've found something," Saff said.

"Maybe. Let's hope their afternoon was less eventful than ours."

CHAPTER TWENTY-FOUR

"*Y*ou found a giant *what?*" Saff asked, eyes wide.

Huon raised an eyebrow at him and repeated himself. "We found an anchor."

"That's not the weirdest thing to have ever ended up on a beach," Fletcher pointed out.

"Trolls don't sail," Tavar said flatly. She'd appeared from the dunes a few minutes before Huon's group. She had looked as frustrated as I felt, until now.

"Neither do Fae," I said.

"Then how…" Fletcher's mouth widened. "Oh. I'm assuming mimicats don't have ships."

"Certainly not," Khat replied. He looked affronted at the very idea. "No self-respecting mimicat would go near water if they could help it, much less *on* it."

"What about you?" Saff asked, barely containing a grin.

Khat flicked his tail and bared his teeth. "Tell me again how you almost drowned. It was such a delightful story."

"Hey." Saff rose to his feet but Huon pressed him back down.

"All right you two," he snapped. "We have enough to deal with without fighting with each other. If you keep at it, I'll toss you both into the sea myself."

Saff flopped back down and crossed his arms. "Fine. Sorry."

Khat gave a last flick of his tail and lay down to groom his ass. "Don't expect an apology," he said around a mouthful of fur.

I shook my head and turned my attention to Huon and Kale. "An anchor on a beach in the Fae realm—"

"Troll territory," Tavar interrupted.

I inclined my head. "On this beach here. It must be a part of this puzzle we're supposed to solve."

"It would be better if they'd left instructions," Fletcher said. "Instead we have this IKEA treasure hunt."

I tilted my head at him. "Who is IKEA?"

"It's a furniture company," he explained. "They sell things in pieces so people have to put them together themselves."

"There must be a lot of carpenters in the human realm," Tavar remarked.

Fletcher shook his head. "Not really. That's kinda the point."

She gave him a confused look, but shrugged and leaned to throw more wood onto the fire she'd built for us.

"Are humans good at puzzles?" I asked.

"Some of them," Fletcher asked. He looked hesitant before he added, "I usually am. Maybe if we can get a look at this anchor, it might make sense."

"It's just an anchor," Huon replied. "I've seen them in the human realm. This one looks no different."

"Except it's here." I rubbed my cheek with my fingertips. "Tavar, have you ever seen anything like it? Maybe the rest of a ship?"

Flames reflected in her eyes when she looked back up at me. I wondered if she got cold without a shirt. Her skin looked thicker and tougher than mine, so perhaps that helped to insulate her. Still, she was braver than me.

She sucked her lower lip between her teeth and

shrugged. "I have found some odd things from time to time, but nothing like this."

"Odd like what?" Kale asked.

"I once found a box of what looked to have been books," she replied. "They were wet and had fallen apart. The box itself was carved in patterns which looked like animals of some kind. Winged ones, but not birds."

"Bats?" Fletcher suggested. "Dragons?"

"I don't know," she replied. "Are those both real things?"

"Bats are," he replied. "As far as I know, dragons aren't."

"Yes, they are," Khat replied.

Fletcher did a double take. "They are?"

"So I've heard." Khat went back to grooming himself.

"Where is this box?" Huon asked.

Tavar replied, "Back at our main camp. I left it with my mothers. They didn't seem to think it had any value, but it was pretty."

"Shit," Huon swore suddenly.

All eyes swung to him.

"What?" I asked.

"You don't see what this might mean?" he asked.

I gave him a blank look.

"If a ship from the human realm came here, the veil might be out in the middle of the ocean," he explained. "Then it sank and debris was washed ashore. Or—" he waved toward Saff "—thrown ashore."

"When I came through, the veil didn't seem that big," Fletcher remarked.

"It's not, " I replied. "That one wasn't, at least. This one might be."

"If a ship can pass through it, it must be huge," Saff said.

"It might explain what happened to Amelia Earhart," Fletcher added.

"Who?" I asked.

"Never mind." He slumped down.

I frowned at him for a moment, but didn't press the question. Instead, I changed the subject. "All right then, I suppose we should get some sleep. Tomorrow might be a long day."

"We *could* sleep," Saff started. He wiggled his eyebrows at me.

"You almost died," I reminded him.

"All the more reason to make the most of my time," he said cheerfully.

"You would all be better off sleeping than screwing," Khat remarked.

"You really seem to object to sex," Saff pointed out.

"I don't object to it, I just prefer to sleep." Khat curled himself up in a ball.

"He is a cat after all," Fletcher said.

Khat cracked open an eye and stared daggers at Fletcher, who held up his hands in surrender.

"The cat has a point though," Huon said. "We should get some rest."

I sighed. "Yes, we all should." I shot Saff an apologetic look and lay back on my blanket. The sand was soft underneath. I wriggled, letting it mould to my body. Truthfully, I was tired and welcomed the chance to lie down and watch the stars twinkle overhead.

"All right, sleep it is," Saff said with a nod.

His response made me smile. I liked a man who could accept no for an answer, without having to press the matter or get sulky. I respected him all the more because he respected me.

"Sleep well," I told him.

"I will. Sweet dreams. Not *too* sweet though," he joked.

I laughed softly and closed my eyes.

*T*ry as I might, I couldn't still my mind.

One by one, the breathing of everyone around me became relaxed and even. Someone—I think it was Huon—began to snore. I rolled over onto my side, then the other one. I tried to sleep on my stomach, but sleep still eluded me.

I couldn't stop thinking about the anchor and wanting to take a look at it.

I chewed my lip. I should contain my curiosity, I knew that, but it still itched at me. Gods, I didn't even know how far down the beach it was.

I sighed and rolled over again.

Finally, unable to relax and not wanting to disturb the others, I rose and crept away from camp.

The moon was full, but partially obscured by clouds. What was visible lit enough of the beach to guide my way.

I walked with one eye on the sand in front of me and another on the tide. It was a long way out now, but I'd already seen how quickly that could change. The gods only knew if it could move faster if it wanted to.

I shook my head. Was I thinking about the ocean as a living thing? Whether it was alive, or the Seafae

Saff claimed to have seen was real, certainly something caused it.

I would continue to be wary of that something.

The clouds drifted and exposed the rest of the moon. The beach was illuminated almost as bright as day.

I stopped to suck in a breath and admire the light sparkling off the ocean. Waves lapped gently at the edge of the shore. If I hadn't seen it a couple of hours ago, I wouldn't have believed it could look so calm and benign.

For a little while, I stood and let my mind wander. Not to the quest we'd found ourselves on, not even to all these incredible men who had surrounded me for the last few days.

Was it only days?

No, I thought about the days before Birch died. The good times before lesser magic was stolen by dark magic. Carefree days and nights of dancing, singing and sitting on a leaf with a book. Nothing mattered back then, at least in comparison to now. Even the arguments with my sisters seemed like petty squabbles that didn't matter any longer.

What had we even argued about? I couldn't remember. A part of me actually missed my sisters. When this was over, I would try to get to know and understand them better. Maybe we could learn to get along somehow.

Maybe mimicats could fly. At least I could try.

A cough sounded behind me. Kale cleared his throat.

I startled and my hand flew to my chest.

"I'm sorry, I didn't mean to scare you," he said, his deep voice a rumble in his chest. "I saw you get up and thought you shouldn't be out here alone."

I hesitated. Part of me was irritated at him having interrupted a quiet moment of introspection. Then the rational side kicked in and reminded me he was right. None of us should be wandering around here by ourselves.

"I couldn't sleep," I admitted. "I was hoping to see the anchor. I might be able to figure it out." I was glad it was too dark for him to see me blush at my own arrogance. If Kale, Tavar and Khat had no idea, then what chance did I have?

Where Huon and maybe Saff would have laughed, Kale just rubbed his chin and nodded.

"It can't hurt to have more eyes and minds on it."

"Really? I mean, of course." My face felt hot.

Kale reached out and took my hand. He gave it a squeeze and said, "You are a smart woman, and more than capable of taking care of yourself. You've proven that time and again. Why do you doubt yourself?"

I looked away, toward the waves. "You're smart. Khat is a smartass. Huon is a king. Fletcher knows all about the human realm." Even though I had been there many times, he had already taught me how little I \knew.

"Tavar seems to know everything you and Khat don't, and Saff is, well, Saff. What does that leave for me?"

Kale pulled me to him gently and wrapped his arms around me. "You're the one who saved Fletcher, more than once. Without you, we wouldn't have found the vault or the first key."

"You would have," I told him. "You're the foretold."

"Foretold or not, you were the anchor. Without you, we might have had to break our way in. You also blasted a hole in the mountain, which is no small feat of magic."

"I suppose so," I said, although now I was squirming. It was my fault for fishing for compliments. Now he was giving them, I felt uncomfortable. All right, I had done a few things, but so had everyone else.

Possibly, deep down, I hoped to be the one to

wield the keys when we found them. After all, Birch set Huon and I on this path. The idea was foolish, I knew that. As long as we got the keys and released lesser magic, it didn't matter who did it.

He put a finger under my chin and turned my face toward him. "You are an asset. We need you. *I* need you." He leaned down and pressed his mouth to mine.

I deepened the kiss and wrapped my arms around his neck. As I did that, I heard a peculiar scratching sound from behind me.

I whirled around to see Khat crouched a few metres away.

Moonlight shone in his eyes as he regarded us, looking unamused, as though we were intruding.

"What?" he asked. "Even a mimicat has to shit." He shook his behind and began to scrape the sand back to cover his business.

"Right." I sighed. "Maybe we should rest anyway. The anchor can wait until morning."

CHAPTER TWENTY-FIVE

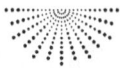

"You're right, it does look ordinary." I wasn't sure what I was expecting, but the anchor was a tarnished piece of metal, half buried under the sand. It had no fancy carvings, nothing to suggest it was anything but a piece of flotsam.

"Can we dig it out?" I asked.

"It's heavy," Huon said, "I tried lifting it yesterday. Maybe between us we could, but Kale suggested we wait."

I looked over to Kale, who looked thoughtful.

"The vault responded to you. I thought if this is related to the key in any way, it might do the same." He pursed his lips and his ear twitched. I hadn't noticed that before, but now I had, I couldn't stop looking. It was so gods damned cute.

"Summer?" Huon interrupted my musing. "Do you want to touch it?"

"Yes," I said, only having half-heard. I blushed. "Oh, the anchor."

Huon broke into a grin. "Yes, the anchor."

"Not that Kale's right ear isn't adorable," Saff interjected.

Kale regarded him with amusement. "Indeed. Anyway, we should hold hands as we did near the vault, in case Summer ends up inside the anchor."

"That would suck," I agreed. From the corner of my eye, I saw Fletcher step closer to the anchor as though he might touch it too.

"Wait!" I said before he could move any closer.

He drew back as though alarmed. "I was just—"

"I know. But you ended up inside the ruins on the other side of the trapdoor, like I did. Kale said if I hadn't been anchored, I would have ended up in the vault. If I can end up inside the anchor, maybe you can too."

"You mean, if we had touched the trapdoor, nothing would have happened?" Huon asked, frowning.

"I have no idea and we don't have time to go back

and check, but if it's possible here, then we should take precautions," I said.

Kale nodded approvingly. "If that's the case, Fletcher might be important somehow."

"Me?" Fletcher looked surprised and disconcerted. "I'm just a human, stuck here by circumstance. It's just by coincidence I ended up there."

"Maybe it is," Huon agreed. "Maybe it's not. We should do what we did with the vault. Me, Summer and Kale. That worked then, it might work again."

"It might not," I said, but I took Huon's hand and he held Kale's. After I sucked in a deep breath and blew it out my nose, I leaned over and pressed my fingertips to the anchor.

Nothing happened.

I waited a minute, two minutes.

I drew back. "That answers that then."

"What about Fletcher?" Saff suggested. "Maybe he can take you—wherever this is supposed to lead."

Everyone turned to Fletcher, who blanched.

"If you're supposed to do this, then there has to be a way out," I reasoned.

"I... suppose so." He swallowed audibly and took Huon's hand. His fingers trembled as he reached toward the anchor. They lightly brushed the tarnished metal before he pressed them against it hard enough to turn his skin white.

I counted to a hundred in my mind before we all dropped hands and stepped away.

"I must say I'm relieved," Huon said. "I didn't really want to end up in there."

I smiled softly and tapped my finger against my lips. "I suppose we should try pulling it out. Maybe there's a riddle engraved on the other end."

"Or this has nothing to do with any puzzles," Khat remarked. He was lying curled up a few metres away, watching us as though he thought us silly for trying any of this.

"Do you have a better idea?" I asked.

He hesitated before saying, "No. I'm just getting bored."

"Well, try to contain yourself a bit longer," I suggested. "Or look around for some alternative."

He swished his tail, but dropped his head onto his paws with a huff. "Fine."

"All right, if we all grab on to a section, we should be able to shift this without too much trouble," Huon said.

"Can't you use magic on it?" Fletcher asked.

"We risk destroying it accidentally," Huon replied.

He cast a sidelong look at me and I smirked in return.

"I don't always blow things up," I retorted.

"Not always, no," he agreed cheerfully.

I gave him a rude gesture with my finger, which he responded to by grinning.

"Anyway," he said after a moment, "we can try this with our hands first. If that doesn't work, we'll resort to magic."

We arrayed ourselves around the anchor and to some unseen cue, put a our hands onto the cold metal. It felt rough under my palm. It must have weathered a lot, even before it ended up here. How many times had it sat on the seafloor, holding its ship in place? How did it come to be here in the first place?

I would probably not get answers to either of those questions.

"One, two, three, push!" Huon directed.

The anchor moved slightly, but the sand held it fast.

"Perhaps we should dig it out?" Tavar suggested.

Huon shook his head, his chin jutted out. "We can do this."

"You don't need to disagree with everything I say, simply because of what I am," she said, her tone curt.

Huon's face reddened.

It was Saff who spoke in his defence. "Huon is a stubborn bastard. He'll dig if we have to, but only if we'd tried his way long enough to know it won't work."

Huon mumbled something. "Come on, let's try again. Push!"

I closed my eyes and pressed against the anchor as hard as I could. My feet sank into the sand as I struggled to keep my footing.

"Push!"

The anchor started to move.

"Push!"

The sand began to fall away from it, dark with moisture down deeper.

With a series of grunts, we shoved the anchor until it fell onto its side on the beach. The moment it hit the ground, it broke into several pieces.

"Rust." Saff poked it with his toes.

"No, it's not." Fletcher stepped forward. "I mean, it is, but rust isn't that even."

I cocked my head. "You're right. Is this a literal puzzle? As in, we put the pieces together and they make something else? That seems too simple."

Fletcher scratched his head. "You're right. There has to be a pattern here."

"It's still more or less anchor-shaped," Saff remarked.

"No shit." Huon poked Saff in the arm.

Saff punched him on the shoulder in return.

"Ouch." Huon rubbed his arm. "I'm pretty sure there are rules about hitting your king."

Saff shrugged, eyes shining with humour. "I like living on the edge."

"Do you want me to throw you both into the ocean?" I tried not to smile at their banter. It was nice, in such difficult times, to have them act their normal, ridiculous, funny selves. Maybe we should be more serious, but the lighter mood made the situation more bearable.

"Only if you're there too," Saff said. "We can make the most of it." He shot me a wink which made my heart flutter.

I rolled my eyes playfully. "That would defeat the purpose of tossing you in."

"You're a hard woman," he teased. He blew me a kiss and only stopped smiling when Tavar gave him a dark look.

"You should focus on the task at hand," she said, her voice tight.

"She's right," I said. "Fletcher, do you have any more clues there?"

He had crouched beside the remains of the anchor. He rested his knee on his thigh and his head on his hand. The sun hit the other side of his face, highlighting his scars. He might hate them, but I found them sexy as hells. They were a sign he'd been through hard times, but he'd survived. Of course, no one deserved to go through anything as terrible as he'd endured, but he had and I adored him for his strength.

"I think some of these pieces would fit together if I tried, but..."

I crouched beside him. "If that's the case, then there's magic involved, and magic is unpredictable and scary as shit."

He turned his eyes to me and the sides of his mouth twitched upward. "Yes, that's pretty much right. How do we know this isn't a trick? You thought the wild tide was caused by dark magic. Just because Saff didn't die doesn't mean you were wrong."

I nodded slowly. "I hadn't thought of that," I admitted. "But we won't know if we don't try." I looked up at the others. "What do you think? Do we do this or not?"

"What's the worst that could happen?" Saff asked.

"We die," Huon replied and shuddered.

"We release dark magic into the realm and end it sooner," Kale said.

"I don't like either of those scenarios," I said.

"It may be that nothing happens," Tavar remarked. "That would be almost as bad. While we waste time here, the realm is slowly dying."

I nodded. As much as I didn't want to die, I didn't want all of this to have been for nothing either.

"Maybe you should stand back," I suggested. "Fletcher and I will try to piece this together."

"Um, Summer." Fletcher's worried tone drew my attention back to him.

"What's wrong?"

"I think we need to hurry." He pointed toward the broken anchor.

Just as the trees had begun to decay, the coating of rust on the metal started to spread.

"If it all falls apart, it could be useless." Fletcher gritted his teeth and reached for a piece.

When he didn't disappear, I did the same. The moment my fingers touched the metal, my skin tingled, like magic recognising magic. I had the strangest sensation that the chunk of former anchor was *happy*.

Clearly, I needed to get more sleep.

I picked up the piece and felt an immediate tug

toward another, which was previously a part of the opposite side of the anchor.

"It's as though it knows where it needs to go," I said, not sure if I should be alarmed or relieved.

"Same with this one," Fletcher said in wonder. "It feels alive, or... something."

"Do we give it what it wants?" The tugging became more insistent.

"I think we have to," he replied. He crab-walked around the sand and placed one piece beside another. With a flash of light and a pop, they melded together. The edges softened until they looked like part of something flat, but circular.

"All right, that wasn't weird at all," I said sarcastically. I followed his example and my piece did the same. Now we had two of what looked like slices of pie.

"I wonder..." Fletcher slid one across the sand toward the other.

The flash was bigger this time, but the pieces melded again until they formed half a circle, with a smooth surface.

"I'm guessing that's not complete." I reached for two more pieces as Fletcher did the same. Two more flashes and we had two more quarter-slices.

"I really think you should stand back," I said over

my shoulder. I heard Huon and Saff's disgruntled muttering, but Kale and Tavar herded them a few metres away. Whether that was far enough remained to be seen.

"Ready?" I looked over to see Fletcher's face, tight, but determined. Of course, if this worked, he could go home. Part of me was happy for him, but my heart ached at the idea of being away from him, after all we had been through in a short amount of time.

What I felt for him was just as strong as what I felt for the three Fae men. Whatever happened, he would always hold a piece of my heart.

"Yes, I'm ready," he replied. "Let's do it." He smiled faintly.

"I give that a nine," I said, and brought the last two pieces of the puzzle together.

CHAPTER TWENTY-SIX

The moment the pieces touched, I braced myself for a blinding flash. I half expected to be knocked back on my ass, or worse.

Instead the pieces bound together and formed a disc with a diameter of about a metre across.

"Is that all?" Fletcher sounded almost disappointed.

"At least the world didn't end," Saff said over my shoulder.

I jumped. "I thought you were staying back?"

"It seems safe enough now," he said.

"Yes, I suppose it does." I eyed the disc as it lay in the sand. I expected it to do something, but it looked like nothing more than a circular chunk of metal. I couldn't even discern any gaps where it had melded itself.

"I'm no expert, but that doesn't look like the veil I came through," Fletcher remarked. "It's just a..." He shrugged.

I took Saff's hand over my shoulder and touched the disc.

Nothing.

"Maybe we need to stand on it?" Huon came up beside Saff. Without waiting for a response, he stepped onto the disc. It rocked slightly and sank into the sand under his weight. A handful of grains covered one side, but slid off when he adjusted his footing.

He held out his hands expectantly, but dropped them when he didn't disappear.

"You might need Summer or Fletcher with you," Saff suggested.

"No," Kale said slowly. "Can you step aside, please." He nodded to Huon.

Huon looked perplexed, but walked off to the side and crossed his arms over his chest.

"What are you thinking?" I asked Kale. "Is the key tugging you at all?"

"It's—" He scratched his temple. "I believe it's

trying to tell me something. We need to flip the disc over."

"Um, all right." It made as much sense as anything else did right now. I gripped a section, while Fletcher did the same. It was heavier than it looked, but we turned it over.

I gasped and dropped the disc. It bore the same symbol as the trapdoor, a rose surrounded by knots.

"All right, this is officially not a coincidence," I declared.

Fletcher murmured his agreement. His face was pale.

"I think we know what we need to do," Kale remarked.

"Oh, you finally figured it out." Khat appeared, winding himself around Saff and Huon's legs for a better look. "It took you long enough."

"I didn't see you helping," Huon remarked darkly.

"I wasn't; I was staying out of the way," Khat said.

"If you had the answer all along, you could have —" I started.

Khat held up a paw. "I didn't, I just thought you were all smart enough to solve it quickly. And you did. Now, we're stepping through, right? Um, maybe one of you should go first?" He backed up a few steps.

"Scaredy-cat," Saff said.

"Damn right," Khat replied. "It means I'm smart."

"Interesting theory," Huon remarked.

"Fuck off," Khat said in Huon's voice.

The king only grinned in response.

"He's right about one thing," Kale said, obviously trying to get the conversation back on track. "We need to decide who is going to the human realm and who isn't."

"I'm going," Fletcher said. "We'll need my help there."

"We?" I asked. I tried to contain the knot of hope in my chest.

He blinked. "Of course. I'm in this to the end. With you." He gave me a soft smile that made my heart flip.

"Me too," Saff said cheerfully. "It's not like I have anything better to do and well..." He blushed as red as his hair. "Summer is pretty amazing."

I blushed then too. "It's my favourite season."

"You're hotter than any summer," he said.

My face was burning. "I... thanks."

"I am also coming," Kale said. "If I am any kind of foretold, then I would assume I have to be involved in some way." He inclined his head toward me. "And I also find myself captivated by you."

"She's going to get a really big head," Huon declared, "but I feel the same way. If I haven't made it clear in the past."

"There have been moments," I agreed. "I thought you hated me for the longest time."

"No, I'm just an idiot who has no idea how to express my feelings." He shrugged with one shoulder.

"That sounds accurate," Saff said. "You've never told me how much you like me either."

"Maybe I don't?" Huon teased.

Saff pouted. "You wound me."

Huon patted him on the shoulder. "You'll live."

"While that's probably true," Kale said, "you, King Huon, should stay here in the Fae realm."

Silence followed that statement.

"I beg your pardon," Huon spluttered. "If you think I'm going to—"

"You *do* have a kingdom to run," I said regretfully.

"I know I do," he replied. "But what sort of king would I be if I sat aside and let you all risk yourselves?"

"An alive one?" Saff suggested. "A smart one?"

"A cowardly one," Huon said, as determined as ever. "I need to do this, to prove I'm worthy of the crown."

"If he wants the respect of the trolls, he should go," Tavar said quietly. She stared Kale down and then added, "I will stay here. Someone will need to guard the veil. I'll have the other bands join me here in doing that. We'll ensure no one follows, or destroys this portal. Besides, I wouldn't go unnoticed in the human realm."

"That's true," I said. "I think having a guard out here would make me feel better anyway."

Tavar nodded and stepped back.

"Have you finished with all your sentimental nonsense?" Khat asked. "Everyone cares about Summer, they all care about her, even Tavar, who is going to cover her ass. Now, can we get going?"

"Are you volunteering to go first now?" Huon asked, looking amused,

"No, I just want you to hurry up," Khat replied. "My kittens await!"

"Are you sure they're yours?" Saff asked. When Khat gave him a filthy look, he grinned.

"I vote he goes first," the mimicat said.

"I think I should go first," Fletcher said. "I'm probably the most dispensable of us."

"*No one* is dispensable," Huon said firmly. "Like it or not, you're one of us now. You might not have wings, but you're our brother." He turned to Saff and Kale. "Right?"

"Yep, you're stuck with us." Saff patted Fletcher's shoulder.

"I agree," Kale said simply.

"See." Huon grinned. "Besides, you're much less annoying than Saff."

"Or Huon," Saff said without missing a beat.

I rolled my eyes. "All right, we all agree. We're all in this together, come what may. However, I think we need to go through together as well." Assuming the disc actually was a portal and led to the human realm. We could be about to descend into the seven hells yet.

I crouched and picked up a handful of sand.

"What are you doing?" Huon asked.

"Just testing a theory," I said. I held my hand over the disc and let the sand trickle between my fingers. When it touched the symbol, it disappeared, as though absorbed by it.

I waited, in case it was spat back like the stick and Saff were. There was no doubt in my mind now that the anchor was tossed onto the beach by the Seafae. Had they kept it safe on the seafloor for a thousand years, waiting for us to come along? The idea that someone had planned all of this was disconcerting, especially if we were chosen in some way.

I always thought prophesies were silly, and best kept in children's stories, but it seemed as though we were living one right now.

What ending did it foretell then? Hopefully a happy one.

"All right, here we go then." I took Fletcher's hand. Huon took the other one. Khat pressed himself against my legs.

I stepped toward the disc in unison with Fletcher, the others right at my back.

I held my breath and stepped onto the symbol. I felt the same tugging sensation as when the pieces of the disc were drawn to each other. This time, however, I was the one being drawn. Down and down, into the disc.

I started to panic a little, but Huon squeezed my hand.

"We can do this." His voice sounded distant, as though he was speaking through a tunnel.

My vision blurred and the beach became a vague wash of yellows and blues. I felt like I was spinning, faster and faster. I became dizzy. Keeping my feet became a challenge.

I bit back a scream.

I heard a voice, but I couldn't make out the words.

"Huon? Fletcher?" My own voice garbled, the words tore away as they left my lips.

Someone called out again, but they sounded far away.

All right, I want to get off this ride now, I thought.

Time wore on. The world spun so quickly I couldn't make out anything but a smudge, interspersed with colour here and there.

My last meal left my stomach and sat in my throat, thick and heavy. I swallowed it back down.

Panic rose again, but this time there was no hand there to comfort me, no sense of having one of my lovers nearby. There was nothing. No one one,

I was alone.

I threw back my head and screamed.

No sound came out.

A tear slid down my cheek and dripped off my chin.

Then everything stopped and I was thrown hard to the ground. I lay there winded for several long moments.

Gradually, I became aware of grass underneath me. I cracked my eyes open. Trees, flowers, a box on a stick of wood. On the box was the number 42.

I lifted my head. A building sat nestled at the edge of the grass. A house. Another sat beside it. And another.

I pushed myself up and sat. "Fletcher? Huon? Saff?" I looked around frantically. "Kale?"

No answer came but the distant barking of a dog.

"Khat?" I said, half to myself. Even his company would have been welcome, but there was no one and no sign of a disc, or anything which hinted at a veil.

I was in the human realm, but I was alone, with no way to know how I would get home, or if I could.

"Well fuck," I muttered.

$\sim$

*W*ill Khat keep cockblocking Summer and Kale? Will they find the second key?

Find out in Glimmer, available now.

ABOUT THE AUTHOR

Maggie Alabaster is a reverse harem and fantasy romance author.

She lives in NSW, Australia with one spouse, two daughters, dog, cat, rabbits and countless birds.

Sign up for my newsletter! Sign Up!

Join my reader group! Join here!

Follow me on Bookbub! Click here to follow me!

ALSO BY MAGGIE ALABASTER

Dark Masque

Book 1 Bait

Book 2 Prey

Book 3 Trap

Saving Abbie

Book 1 Pitch

Book 2 Pound

Book 3 Session

Book 4 Muse

Book 5 Rhythm

Book 6 Encore

Novella Venomous

Ruthless Claws

Book 1 Ivory

Book 2 Crimson

Book 3 Elodie

Harmony's Magic

Book 1 Summoned by Fire

Book 2 Summoned by Fate

Book 3 Summoned by Desire

Shifter's Vault

Book 1 Discarded

Book 2 Deceived

Book 3 Disgraced

My Alien Mates

Book 1 Star Warriors

Book 2 Star Defenders

Book 3 Star Protectors

Academy of Modern Magic

Book 1 Digital Magic

Book 2 Virtual Magic

Book 3 Logical Magic

Complete Collection

Summer's Harem

Book 1: Shimmer

Book 2: Glimmer

Book 3: Flicker

Complete collection

Short reads

Taken by the Snowmen

Jingle All the Way

Also by Maggie Alabaster and Erin Yoshikawa

Caught by the Tide

Book 1–Pursued by Shadows

Book 2 Pursued by Darkness

Book 3 Pursued by Monsters